HIGH SCHOOL MUSICAL

STORIES FROM EAST HIGH #8

GET YOUR VOTE ON!

By Beth Beechwood and N. B. Grace

Based on the Disney Channel Original Movie
"High School Musical," Written by Peter Barsocchini
Based on "High School Musical 2," Written by Peter Barsocchini
Based on Characters Created by Peter Barsocchini

Bath New York Singapore Hong Kong Cologne Delhi Melbourne

First published by Parragon in 2008
Parragon
Queen Street House
4 Queen Street
Bath BA1 1HE, UK

ISBN 978-1-4075-2576-1

Printed in the UK

CHAPTER ONE

Troy Bolton and Sharpay Evans sat next to each other in the boardroom near Principal Matsui's office, staring at a group of people whose lips seemed to be moving in slow motion. It was a school-board meeting and it was even more boring than it had sounded earlier that day, when Principal Matsui had suggested they attend. He hadn't even told them why they both had to be there. Even worse, it was a Friday afternoon! Their weekend should already have started—instead, they were listening to people drone on about approving budget numbers, hiring an assistant school nurse, upcoming parent-teacher meetings. . . .

I can't believe I missed basketball practice for this, Troy thought.

I can't believe I missed *Inside the Actors Studio* for this, thought Sharpay.

Troy started to jiggle his leg with impatience, causing his chair to shake. The Wildcats had a big game coming up, and this was not a good time to be observing the bureaucratic process. Principal Matsui shot Troy a look. Troy made an apologetic face and immediately stopped bouncing.

"Now, on to the renovations budget," Mr. Griffith, the head of the board, said. "Mr. Bolton, Ms. Evans, would you please stand?"

Troy and Sharpay exchanged nervous glances. What could this possibly have to do with them? Reluctantly, they both stood up.

"We have found some money in the budget

that will cover the renovation of either the gymnasium or the auditorium," Mr. Griffith said.

Troy's eyes brightened. A new gym? This was great news! If he tripped over that loose floor plank on the way from the bench to the court one more time, he thought he was going to scream.

Sharpay's heart raced. A revamped auditorium? How fabulous! Her thoughts went immediately to a giant sign with her name in lights. One of these days, East High was going to realize what a star they had on their hands—and the installation of a huge, showstopping sign was the first step in making sure that happened!

Their thoughts were interrupted by Mr. Griffith clearing his throat and adding, "Unfortunately, we don't have enough money to renovate both areas. That means we're going to have to make a hard choice."

Troy and Sharpay looked at each other smugly.

"Still, it's great that East High gets any renovations at all," Troy said diplomatically. Of course, he thought, it's obvious the gym needs to be renovated more than the auditorium.

Not to be outdone, Sharpay added cheerfully, "Yes, it's really wonderful! But how will you choose between two such worthy projects?" The choice was actually quite simple, she thought. After all, the auditorium was always filled with the magic of theater, while the gym was always filled with . . . sweaty people.

Troy wanted to roll his eyes at her supersweet tone, but he didn't. After all, he was dying to know, too.

"That's a very good question," Mr. Griffith said. "In fact, the school board decided that this decision offers a great opportunity to demonstrate the power of the vote. For that reason, we're going to let the student body choose which area should be renovated. Principal Matsui suggested that you two would be the best people to organize election campaigns and get students excited about participating in the democratic process. Starting on Monday, you will have one week to campaign for your cause. We'll hold the vote next Friday afternoon at two p.m. That will give you five days to campaign."

Sharpay had barely listened after he had uttered the word "vote." She was picturing herself delivering a speech that would end all speeches. She would be passionate, convincing, and charismatic—and that giant sign in lights would be hers!

"Ms. Evans?" Mr. Matsui bumped her elbow lightly to bring her attention back to the meeting. "Mr. Griffith was speaking to you."

"Oh, sorry, sir!" Sharpay said. "My wheels are already spinning, trying to figure out the best and most honest way to run my campaign."

Troy let out a sigh. He knew this was going to be a long, competitive week.

"Well, that's good to hear, young lady. We're looking forward to seeing the campaigning process. As I was saying, keep it clean and fun, and try to get other students involved."

Principal Matsui stood up and put one hand

on Troy's shoulder and another on Sharpay's. "You can count on these two to run fine campaigns, sir." He beamed.

With that, Mr. Griffith adjourned the meeting, and the room rustled with the sound of people putting away papers. Principal Matsui stopped Troy and Sharpay from leaving right away, though. "I know you will both keep the antics to a minimum and make sure East High comes out looking like a winner in the end," he said in a serious tone. Mr. Matsui was always very concerned with appearances, and this was an opportunity to really impress the school board. Both Troy and Sharpay understood this.

"Of course, sir." Troy nodded confidently.

"Naturally," Sharpay said before adding, "but the Drama Club will be the *real* winner." She raised her eyebrows at Troy and said, "See you on the campaign trail!" as she skipped happily out of the room.

Troy guessed that she was running home to

tell her brother, Ryan, the news. Then they would probably call an emergency late-night meeting of the Drama Club to get an early jump on things. As he left the boardroom, he realized he'd better get a move on if he was going to compete with Sharpay.

Troy made a beeline for the gym. Practice would be over, but usually some of the team members hung out in the locker room afterward. Sure enough, when he opened the door, he found them sitting in the bleachers, going over every detail of practice. Hanging with the guys was always more fun than going home to study.

"Hey! How was the big board meeting, Mr. Bolton?" Chad Danforth asked when he saw Troy walk in.

"Actually," Troy said, grabbing a seat, "it started out pretty mind-numbing, but I have to say it got extremely interesting later on."

"How could a school-board meeting possibly be interesting?" asked Zeke Baylor.

"Well, as it turns out, there is some money in

the budget for a big renovation project, and . . ."
Troy paused for dramatic effect, ". . . either the
gym *or* the auditorium will get it."

"Awesome!" Chad exclaimed.

"What do you mean, 'either'?" Zeke asked.

"Well, that's the thing," Troy said. "There's
going to be a schoolwide election. We have to run
a campaign and see who gets the most votes."

They all looked at Troy, calculating what this
meant.

"Of course, we'll win!" Troy said confidently.

"Sure! We've got it in the bag. We're the
basketball team. Although we *are* running
against Sharpay," Chad said.

"Oh, I know," Troy agreed. "And I'm sure
she's already plotting away. She ran out of the
meeting in such a hurry, there's no way she and
Ryan aren't building their campaign as we
speak."

"Hey, Troy," Jason Cross called out, "if we
win, we can get that new floor!"

"That was the first thing I thought of!" Troy

exclaimed. It was annoying to the whole team that the floor was in such bad shape. After all, they were champions! They deserved floorboards that didn't buckle.

"So," Troy continued, "I just wanted to let you guys know what was up. I'll call Gabriella tonight and make sure she and Taylor and the Scholastic Decathlon team are on board. Okay, everybody think about what we can do for our campaign over the weekend, and we'll meet on Monday to get this thing going."

"Right on," Zeke said, putting his hand out in front of the group, as they would in a team huddle. The others did the same, and soon it was a pile-on of hands.

"Let's do this!" Troy shouted, and they all broke away, cheering.

When Troy got home, he sat down for a quick dinner. He was eager to get upstairs and call Gabriella Montez. He knew she would have some good ideas and be really excited about the possibility of the gym getting renovated.

"Hey, Gabriella," Troy said when he heard her on the line.

"Hi, Troy," she answered, clearly happy to hear his voice. "How was the big meeting?"

Troy told her all about the renovation project, and how he and Sharpay were going to be running opposing campaigns. When he was finished explaining, he didn't exactly get the encouragement he was hoping for.

"Hmm," Gabriella replied. "So the school board has already narrowed the choice down to either the gym or the theater?"

"Well, yeah," he said. "I guess they thought that since basketball games and musicals are the two biggest student draws, it would make the most sense to use the money there."

"I guess that's one way to look at it," Gabriella said slowly.

"Hey, I thought you'd really be into this," Troy said, surprised by her lack of enthusiasm. "You know, rockin' the vote, getting down with the political process, learning how government works. Plus, how great will it be when we win? I can just see the look on Sharpay's face."

"That's great, Troy. Can't wait to see how it all unfolds," Gabriella said briskly. "But I need to go. I have a lot of homework."

"Wait," Troy interrupted. "I wanted to ask if you and Taylor would join the gym campaign. With the two of you on our side, I'm sure we'd win by a landslide."

"Sure, I guess we can help out," she said nonchalantly. Then, in an obvious ploy to change the subject, she said, "Hey, did you still want to go to a movie this weekend? There are a couple that I'd love to see. . . ."

They talked for another twenty minutes about weekend plans and then hung up. The school election wasn't mentioned again.

After Gabriella said good-bye, Troy stared at the receiver he held in his hand. When he had told her about being chosen to run the campaign for the gym, he had expected her to be bubbling over with enthusiasm, the way she normally was.

Maybe she was just feeling stressed about a big test or something, he thought as he hung up the phone. He needed to hit the books himself. He wanted to get a jump-start on his schoolwork this weekend so he could spend most of his free time next week running his campaign.

CHAPTER TWO

On Monday morning, Troy couldn't wait to get the campaign started! He was meeting his friends during lunchtime to discuss their strategies. As he sat slouched in his chair, doodling ideas in his notebook, he was startled to hear Sharpay's voice over the loudspeaker during homeroom announcements.

"Good morning, my fellow students!" she shouted. "This is Sharpay Evans—everyone's favorite East High icon. Wondering what I'm up to now? Well, I'm running a campaign for your vote. Yes, *you!*" she said cheerfully. "Ever sit in the auditorium, wishing you could see close-ups of your favorite performers? Maybe on a big screen? In *high-definition*? Well, your wishes could come true this Friday! Just cast your vote in favor of renovating the auditorium, and you will get all that and more! In fact—"

"Okay, Ms. Evans," Principal Matsui quickly interrupted. "Thank you for your announcement."

The students heard a screech of feedback as someone took the microphone away from the principal. Then Ryan's voice boomed out of the PA: "We are the Drama Club, and we approve this message!"

There was another screech as the principal got control of the microphone again. "As I was saying," he went on, "I'd like to thank Ms. Evans for her announcement—"

Troy was fuming. He couldn't believe Sharpay had gotten to work so fast! He was annoyed with Mr. Matsui for allowing her to use his announcement time for her campaign. And he was even more annoyed with himself that he hadn't thought of it first!

"I'd also like to point out that what you've just heard was a campaign speech," Mr. Matsui said. "There will be a vote on Friday, and Sharpay Evans and Troy Bolton will campaign to convince you to vote for renovating either the auditorium or the gym. So, in the interest of fairness, Mr. Bolton will have his chance to make a short speech during tomorrow's announcements. Looking forward to a well-fought but clean campaign all around!"

Immediately, Troy felt much better.

Sharpay, however, was irritated. Back in Mr. Matsui's office, she shot him a look. "Hold on," she said. "Making a speech during announcements was *my* idea."

"And it was a good one, Sharpay," Mr. Matsui agreed. "But I have to give equal airtime to *both* campaigns. You understand that, don't you?" He finished with a smile.

Sharpay understood the concept of fairness, at least in theory, but she was never happy when it was applied to her. She had been so pleased when she came up with this idea the previous night, while she and Ryan had watched *The American President* on TV.

"Fine," she huffed. "At least I was first. I'm sure that made quite an impression on everyone at East High."

With that, Sharpay stalked off. She had lots of other ideas, and she couldn't waste any time on this. She had done what she came to do—the campaign was on!

When the bell rang for the next class, Troy walked down the hall, doing his best to listen to what the electorate—that is, his fellow students—was saying. He was disappointed to discover that most people were gossiping about what they had done over the weekend. The few comments he *did* hear about the election were disheartening. Some people, apparently, had already been won over by the promise of a huge plasma TV screen in the auditorium.

"That would be incredible!" one girl exclaimed. "So twenty-first century!"

"I don't know," said a guy standing next to her. "I have a feeling we'll be seeing a lot of close-ups of Sharpay Evans—"

"Yeah, but still! It will make going to the auditorium so much more fun!" she replied. "You know, more like going to the movies!"

"I guess you're right," her friend agreed as they moved out of earshot.

Suddenly, Troy spotted Chad. He was especially happy to see him at that moment, since he had just gotten very nervous about the possibility of losing the vote. Chad was with Zeke and Jason; the three of them headed across the hall and gave Troy high fives.

Troy sighed. "You know what, guys? I think this campaign is going to be tougher than I counted on."

"It's Sharpay, dude!" Chad exclaimed. "Like I said, you can't underestimate the girl."

"Nah, we have this in the bag," Jason said confidently. "No one is going to vote to fix up an auditorium instead of a gym!"

"That's right," Zeke chimed in. "It's just not going to happen."

"I don't know," Chad said. "Now all I can think about is seeing every pore on your face during your next big show."

Troy gave his friend a quick fake punch to the ribs. Chad blocked him, laughing.

"Very funny," Troy said dryly. "Look, I know you're joking, but it's time for us to get serious about this election or we'll be tripping on the loose board in the gym until we graduate. Don't forget about our first campaign meeting at lunch today—Gabriella and Taylor are in, too."

Chad gave him a pat on the back. "We'll figure something out. Don't worry," he said as he walked away.

Why would I be worried? Troy thought. Jason's right. We've got this in the bag.

But by the time lunch rolled around, Troy was

thoroughly annoyed. Sharpay had already put up posters in the hall—bright, colorful, *huge* posters. He felt three steps behind, and he knew from playing basketball that that was not a good place to be.

He was relieved to see Gabriella, Taylor McKessie, and his teammates waiting for him in the cafeteria. Gabriella hadn't sounded very psyched about the election and hadn't mentioned it all weekend. He had been a little afraid that she wouldn't even show up. But she was chatting with Chad, and seemed as positive and friendly as ever.

Troy walked toward the group, smiling. He thought it was important to project an air of confidence, even if he wasn't totally feeling that way. He took a seat next to Gabriella, who smiled at him, but still seemed a little distant. Troy put his arm around her shoulders and noticed that her body tensed up. Something was definitely up. "Are you all right?" he asked.

"Fine," she replied, a fake smile plastered on

her face. What she felt like saying was, *No, Troy, I'm not all right. I'm sick of everything in this school being about either the basketball team or the Drama Club. The Scholastic Decathlon team could always use the extra money, too!*

Gabriella took a deep breath. She knew she had to sit through this brainstorming meeting and nod and be cheerful because that was what everyone expected of her. The problem was, she just wasn't feeling that enthusiastic.

Troy turned his attention to the group. He wanted to know what was going on with Gabriella, but right now, he had to focus. "Okay," he began. "What's first?"

"We need a slogan, man," Chad urged.

"*And* we need a platform," Taylor pointed out. "People need to know what they'll get if they vote for us."

"Yeah, what are we going to use the money for, Troy?" Zeke asked. "Besides refinishing the floor, which is a given."

"I think we should get a new scoreboard, for

starters," Troy said, and they all nodded in agreement. At least a third of the lights were always burned out on the current one.

"Great idea!" Zeke exclaimed. Then, getting into the spirit of things, he added, "You know what else would be cool? Banners to honor some of East High's past greats!"

Chad nodded enthusiastically and added with a smirk, "Not to mention the *current* stars."

"Yeah!" Troy cheered. "And there should be a big banner celebrating our championship, too," he added.

"Hold on, you guys," Gabriella piped up now, with a hint of anger in her voice. "I wouldn't be so sure that you're going to win this election if I were you. Just because the basketball team is so popular doesn't necessarily mean students will vote for you. Sometimes, it's all about the underdog, and Sharpay, like it or not, is the underdog here. Just think of all the political upsets throughout history. When President Truman was reelected in 1948, no one saw it coming, especially his opponent!" She gave them a warning look. "We don't want that to happen to us."

"Okay, Anderson Cooper," Chad said sarcastically, referring to the TV news analyst. "I'm pretty sure this one's in the bag, but we sure do appreciate your optimism!"

"I'm just saying that those who don't learn from history are doomed to repeat it," she countered.

"You have a good point," Troy said. "We don't want to take anything for granted. Gabriella, what would you suggest we do?"

Calming down, she gave him a small smile. "Well, I do have a few ideas. . . ."

As Troy's group continued to toss around plans during lunch, Sharpay sat across the cafeteria with her own team. She had called upon Ryan, of course, to act as the campaign manager. She had also invited Alicia Thomas and Charlotte Richards from the Drama Club. She was reluctant to include Ashley Appleton in her campaign, because Sharpay was beginning to suspect that Ashley had a little crush on Troy. But she needed all the help she could get and figured that it would be better to have Ashley working for her than for Troy.

She even asked Eugene, the technical wizard who helped with lighting and sound on all the musicals, to be a part of the team. After all, Eugene was a behind-the-scenes kind of guy—and she had noticed that there was someone like that in almost every election movie that she had seen.

"Welcome to the winning campaign," Sharpay announced. Everyone greeted this confident invitation with light applause. "We are well on our way to getting a new light and sound system—"

"*Yesss!*" Eugene jumped up and pumped his fist in the air with excitement. Sharpay gave him a freezing glance, and he sheepishly sat down again.

"As I was saying," she continued, "we will also get the revamped dressing rooms we all deserve so much. Picture it," she said. "Spalike rooms for the stars of the show, painted in Zen colors, complete with piped-in music and waterfalls to relax us and keep us happy."

She looked up to see the group staring at her imaginary image with smiles on their faces. "Don't get any ideas, people. *I* will be the star." Their faces fell. "But you know I would never forget the little people," she said graciously. "You will all have a common area with music and nice paint, too!"

Alicia and Charlotte perked up at a break in Sharpay's monologue. "Oh, and new chairs for the audience!" Alicia exclaimed.

"Yeah, those current ones make your butt hurt after a while," Charlotte agreed.

Ryan interrupted. He felt that someone needed to point out the obvious. "We haven't won *yet*," he said, "and basketball is pretty popular at this school. We're going to have to really sell the idea of renovating the auditorium."

"Ryan," Sharpay said through clenched teeth,

"as campaign manager I expect you to exude confidence, optimism, and a firm conviction that we will not lose. After all, putting on a winning election campaign is just like putting on a successful show—and no one knows how to do that better than the Drama Club!"

Everyone murmured in agreement as Ryan looked down. "Sorry, Sharpay," he said.

When the meeting was adjourned, everyone scattered to post more signs and rally support for their campaign.

Ashley caught up with Ryan as they left the cafeteria. "This is going to be great, Ryan. The auditorium really does need the renovation."

"I hope so," he said, and then caught himself. "I mean, yes, you're absolutely right!" He gave her a shy glance. Ryan had developed a little crush on Ashley since she had arrived at East High, although he hadn't had the nerve to do anything about it. "And thanks for helping us out, by the way."

"No problem! Sharpay has been so good to

me; I really just want to give something back. Besides, I haven't ruled out politics as a future career, so this will be good experience!" Ashley paused, her head tilted to one side. "You know, Ryan, you didn't share any ideas on how to use the money. Is something wrong?"

Ryan debated telling her what he had been thinking. He decided he needed to share his concern—maybe Ashley would help him figure out what to do about it. "Well, it's just that I overheard Principal Matsui talking to Sharpay after this morning's announcements. He said she shouldn't have promised a plasma-screen TV, because it may be too expensive. I don't know much about politics, but I know it's not a good idea to get elected by promising things you can't deliver. It could end up hurting our campaign." Ryan felt better the moment he said this out loud to Ashley. It was really bothering him, and he was glad to have someone to talk to.

"Oh . . ." Ashley said slowly. "I see. Yeah, I could see where you might be worried about that.

Well, you know what? We don't *know* that they won't let us have a plasma-screen TV, so it wasn't really a lie," she offered.

"That's true! I hadn't thought of that!" Ryan exclaimed. "Thanks, Ashley. I'm really glad I mentioned it to you."

"You're welcome," she replied. "Well, time to go put up some posters! See you around."

"Yes, definitely," Ryan said. "See you later!"

They headed off in opposite directions—Ryan to algebra and Ashley in search of Troy.

Wait until Troy hears this, Ashley thought gleefully.

CHAPTER THREE

After their campaign meeting ended, Troy caught up with Gabriella as she walked out of the cafeteria. He had to know what was going on with her. "Gabriella," he said, touching her arm, "I can tell something is bothering you, and I'm not going to let you go until you tell me what's up."

Gabriella glanced down the hall, wishing she could get out of the conversation. "Honestly, Troy, it's nothing."

"Gabriella, I know you're lying," he said.

"One, because I know you really well. And two, because you're a terrible liar."

She couldn't help laughing at that, and Troy smiled back. "Come on," he coaxed. "Please tell me what's wrong."

Gabriella sighed. "Well, it's just that I feel like everything at this school is always about you and the basketball team or Sharpay and the Drama Club," she admitted. "I guess I just wish I played a bigger role in things."

"Gabriella, you are the prettiest, smartest, most talented girl East High has ever seen. The only reason you feel left out is because you're so good at everything. You don't have to focus on just one thing, like me or Sharpay."

Gabriella smiled. Troy was being really nice. She had expected him to be defensive. "Is this part of your new campaign personality?" she joked.

"Yes," he said, smiling. "My name is Troy Bolton. Can I count on your vote?"

Gabriella was laughing again. "I'm sorry, Troy. I don't know what's gotten into me.

Anyway, the gym *should* get the renovation—so many teams use the space, and so many events are held there. It's the better choice."

"See, this is why I need your help—you know just the right angle to play!" he said, putting his arm around her as they walked down the hallway.

"Thanks, Troy." Gabriella smiled. "Speaking of which . . . Can we meet after basketball practice? I have an idea I want to talk to you about."

"You bet! See you then." Troy walked away feeling much better about everything.

Gabriella hurried to class—she wanted to get there early, because she hoped to put her plan into action before the end of the day.

Later that afternoon, Ashley waited outside the locker room for Troy. She looked at her watch nervously. She didn't want to run into Sharpay and have to explain why she was there.

"Hey, Ashley," Troy said. "What are you doing

here?" Troy was not a huge fan of Ashley, as she had a habit of talking about people behind their backs. Especially Gabriella's.

Ashley jumped. She had been so anxious about running into Sharpay that her nerves had gotten the best of her. "Hey," she squeaked.

"Didn't mean to scare you," Troy said. "What are you doing here?" he asked casually.

"Oh, just some campaign stuff for Sharpay. To be honest, I think she wanted me to scope out the gym area to see if she could find out what you guys were up to."

"Oh, really?" Troy asked. "So you're working on Sharpay's campaign? Well, I guess I better watch what I say around you."

"That's right," Ashley said, moving in to touch Troy's arm.

"Listen," Troy said, eager to change the subject. "Have you seen Gabriella? We're supposed to meet here." Just then Gabriella came around the corner and saw Troy talking with Ashley.

Ugh, Gabriella thought, when she spotted

them. She didn't trust Ashley for one second.

As Gabriella approached, Ashley took a step away from Troy. "Hi, Gabriella," she said nervously.

"Hi, Ashley," Gabriella said coolly.

"Well, I'm off," Ashley said, looking over at Troy. "Now that the plasma-screen is probably a bust, we have to come up with a new strategy." She winked in Troy's direction as she said these last words, then turned on her heel and walked off with a little wave.

Gabriella gave Troy a questioning look.

"So the Drama Club can't promise a super-state-of-the-art screen after all," Troy said thoughtfully. "That's going to put a kink in their campaign."

Gabriella rolled her eyes. "You *know* Ashley came here on purpose to tell you that, Troy."

"You think so?" he asked, surprised. "It seemed like she just let it slip out."

"Troy, do you think she just happened to be hanging around outside the gym after school?"

she said, shaking her head. "No way. She was waiting to run into you and let you in on their little problem."

"Well, so far her plan to woo me with inside information is a total failure," Troy said.

"So far?" Gabriella asked, one eyebrow raised.

Troy and Gabriella looked at each other and laughed.

Just then, Chad, Zeke, and Jason walked out of the locker room.

"Hey, Gabriella," Chad said. "Troy said you had a big idea you wanted to tell us about. So . . . ?"

"Hold on," she called, as she ran back down the hallway. They could hear her talking to someone around the corner. It sounded as if she was being very persuasive.

When she returned, she was dragging someone with her. It was Nathan James—the neurotic, test-obsessed guy who had driven them all crazy at SAT time.

"Okay," Gabriella said, "I know you're all

wondering why I've brought Nathan here to help with the campaign to get the gym renovated."

"Um, *yeah*," Chad said. "No offense, Nathan, but you don't seem like the kind of guy who even knows where the gym *is*."

Nathan scowled at him through his wire-rimmed glasses. "For your information," he said stiffly, "there is more to me than a razor-sharp memory and a brilliant intellect. I've also practiced the martial art known as tai chi for the last seven years, in order to enhance my mind-body connection, which has led me, on occasion, to the gym. And furthermore—"

"Furthermore, I decided that what we really need to win this election is a pollster," Gabriella interrupted hastily. "Someone who will interview people and find out what they're thinking about the issues, how they intend to vote, and how we can make the best case to convince them to vote for us. That will give us the edge we need, and Nathan is just the right guy to do it."

"Indeed," Nathan agreed. "Go, team!"

"Let me get this straight," Chad questioned curiously. "You want to help the *basketball team*? Since when?"

"Hey, come on, Chad," Troy said. "Gabriella's right; we can use the help—"

"If I may answer the question?" Nathan quickly interrupted. "I have no interest in helping you all get new helmets or whatever. I'm doing this for a very practical reason. Taking on a project like this could make all the difference on my college applications." His eyes glittered with the maniacal fervor that had become all too familiar during their SAT-prep classes. "It will add that extra dimension that will make me stand out from the crowd of average applicants. In fact, it could very well make me the most sought-after high school senior in the country!"

The basketball players exchanged doubtful glances. This guy was wound just a little bit too tightly. How was he going to help them win?

Gabriella sensed their hesitation and quickly stepped in on Nathan's behalf. "No one's smarter or more thorough than Nathan. And Taylor's going to work with Nathan on the polling. I think they'll do a great job. Now, let's all get to the art room—we have some posters to make!" she finished cheerfully.

But when they got to the art room, they found Sharpay, Ryan, and some of the set designers from the Drama Club already hard at work. As confident as Troy was, he was a little dismayed to see the posters they were making. There was no way the basketball team could compete with Sharpay's crew when it came to art.

Gabriella noted Troy's expression.

"Wow, Sharpay!" Gabriella exclaimed. "Your signs are fabulous. We really have our work cut out for us." She was being over the top with her compliment, and Sharpay knew it.

"*We*?" Sharpay asked. "You know, Gabriella, you should come over to work for our side. You don't really think Troy's team is going to win the election, *do* you?"

Gabriella smiled politely. "Of course I do!"

she exclaimed. "And I think the rest of the students will agree when they cast their votes on Friday," she added.

"Well, we'll see about that," Sharpay said haughtily, gathering a bunch of signs. "You and your *winning* team better get a move on. You can't run on your precious basketball championship forever. We got our message out first during this morning's announcements, we've got posters up everywhere, *and* we've already started to build a buzz. Face it, we're already way ahead of you—and that's just the beginning."

With that, she stormed out, leaving the rest of her team behind. Ryan and the other Drama Club members looked at each other and shrugged. It seemed odd for Sharpay just to take off like that, but they had learned not to question her.

Two seconds later, Sharpay marched back in and grabbed Ryan by the arm. "Let's *go*, people!" she shouted. Her campaign team shuffled out behind her. Gabriella, Troy, Chad, and Zeke giggled softly.

"Well, guys," Gabriella said once only pro-gym-campaign members remained, "Sharpay's right about one thing. We can't just assume we'll win. We have to get out there and hit the hallways with our message."

"Which is?" Chad asked.

"Get your vote on!" Gabriella said, cheering.

They all laughed and gave each other high fives. The campaign was on!

CHAPTER FOUR

By Tuesday morning, East High was completely transformed. Giant posters for both campaigns were plastered everywhere. Sharpay was busy stopping students she had never met before to chat about her cause.

"What exactly are you hoping for from the auditorium renovation?" she eagerly asked one unsuspecting freshman.

Sharpay had stayed up late the night before watching famous political speeches in order to hone her campaigning style. As usual, she gave 110 percent—which meant that her style was just a *little* too forceful. The student she had accosted gave her a scared look and hurried away. Sharpay rolled her eyes. What was with these kids today? she thought. Didn't they know their vote could make a difference . . . in *her* life?

Troy, meanwhile, was also campaigning in the hallway, although he took a more low-key approach. As students rushed around him on their way to class, he announced, "We need your vote. Without the fans, the basketball team is just a bunch of guys bouncing a ball around. With the fans, we *are* school spirit; we *are* East High."

But even that seemed to fall on deaf ears. Troy and Sharpay exchanged glances, almost sympathetic to each other's cause for a moment. But then they looked away. The moment had passed.

Gabriella came running up to Troy with Nathan in tow. "Troy!" She gasped. "Nathan has some news to report. Can we talk in private?"

"What have we here?" Sharpay interrupted. "What is Nathan doing for you, Troy?"

"He's just helping out behind the scenes," Troy said casually. "No big deal." He certainly didn't want Sharpay to get any ideas about stealing Nathan away. . . .

But it was already too late. If there was one thing Sharpay knew, it was how to compete, and she had immediately sensed that Nathan might somehow offer Troy's team an advantage, even if she wasn't quite sure how.

"Oh, really?" Sharpay asked. "How very interesting!" She turned her megawatt smile on Nathan. "But why do you want to help get the gym fixed up? You're so smart and cultured and, um, *smart*. I would think you would have a natural affinity for the theater!"

"Back off, Sharpay," Troy said in frustration. "Nathan's working for us."

"You may have gotten to him first, but he can still switch teams," she snapped. "If he wants to work for the *winning* team, that is."

Troy opened his mouth to respond, but before he could say anything, Nathan held up his hand.

"Actually," he said, "I'm not working for *either* campaign."

Troy and Sharpay both stared at him.

"I," Nathan said solemnly, "am working for the people."

There was a brief silence. Then Sharpay exploded. "The people?" she yelled. "Who cares about the people?"

"We do," Gabriella said firmly. "Because the voters are the ones in charge, not the politicians. And that's what I've been trying to tell you. The problem is that the people don't care about *us*."

"What do you mean?" Troy asked.

"I'll explain," Nathan interrupted. He opened his briefcase and pulled out a spreadsheet. "My initial poll indicates that there is widespread apathy about this election among the student body."

"In other words?" Sharpay asked sharply.

"In other words," Nathan said, "they're not going to vote for either of you. They just don't care very much."

Sharpay furrowed her brow. But I'm so interesting, she thought. How could this be?

"Why not?" she demanded.

"Yeah, and what can we do to make them want to vote?" Troy added.

"I'm on it," Nathan declared. "That's my next poll." He hurried away, furiously scribbling in his notebook.

"Come on, Troy," Gabriella said, tugging at his arm. "We have a lot of work to do. We should really get going."

"Yes, you two go on and put your heads together," Sharpay urged. "I'm sure you'll come up with something great." They looked at her suspiciously, but she had already turned on her heel and walked away. She had an important rehearsal to get to. After all, she was determined to win the campaign, and she didn't have one minute to waste!

* * *

Moments later, Sharpay found Ryan, Ashley, and the rest of the Drama Club waiting for her in the auditorium.

"Okay, people," Sharpay shouted. "What did I just hear? East High doesn't care about the election! So what are we going to do? We're gonna make them care! And how will we do that?"

Thinking Sharpay was going to answer her own question yet again, the group remained silent. Sharpay silently counted to five and then yelled, "I said, 'How will we do that?'"

Ryan jumped. Oh! She wanted to hear from them!

"In a way that only the Drama Club can!" he cried out. "Wait till you guys hear the song I wrote for us to sing!"

"Wait—what are you talking about?" Ashley asked. "Nobody said I was going to have to sing."

"Oh, don't worry, Ashley," Sharpay reassured her. "People will only be listening to me. You guys are just my backup. Today at lunchtime, we're gonna rock the cafeteria! Then we'll see about this apathy Nathan was talking about."

Just then, a loud screech of feedback came from the loudspeaker. After a few moments, the screeching stopped and Principal Matsui said, "Good morning, East High students! I have a quick update on the election. As you all know, the school board did find funds for school reno-vation—but the funds are not limitless. In other words, I'm sorry to say that, after pricing the plasma-screens used in theaters, we will not be able to afford one, no matter who wins." He cleared his throat and added, "However, don't let that dampen your enthusiasm for voting! There is still a choice to be made, and you, the students of East High, are the ones who will make it!"

After making a few more brief announce-ments, the principal signed off.

Sharpay shot a look at Ryan. "Your song better be good," she warned.

"Have I ever let you down, sis?" Ryan asked.

The group got right to work and agreed to memorize the words to the song so that they'd be ready to perform it by lunchtime. They knew they could handle it. After all, they *were* pros, and Ryan had already given the music to the band members so that they would have plenty of time to learn it.

Ashley had history class with Troy before lunch, and she was eager to see him again. She hoped that giving him a little inside information would make him understand she was serious about him. She made sure she arrived to class early and cornered Troy before most of the other students had arrived.

"Hey, Troy," she said coyly. "How's your campaign going?"

"Great," he said. "But we need to get some election fever going in this school!"

"I know, I heard." She shook her head sadly. "Whatever happened to the spirit of civic participation? I don't get it. Doesn't everyone know how important it is to vote?"

"That's what I think, too," Troy said. True, he didn't trust Ashley. After all, she was working with Sharpay. And, to be truthful, he hadn't been one of her biggest fans when she had transferred to East High. But he was happy to hear someone, *anyone*, in the school talk about the election as if it meant something. He had just spent his study break trying to drum up support for his cause among the student body, and he'd been met with nothing but indifference. Just thinking about it made him fume. "You know what one kid just said to me?" he asked Ashley, his voice rising. "He said that it didn't matter if he voted, because everybody *else* would vote!"

"No!" Ashley opened her eyes wide, trying to look shocked. "Doesn't he even care whether it's the gym or the auditorium that gets renovated? That's an extremely important decision!"

"That's what I said!" Troy exclaimed. Maybe Ashley wasn't so bad after all, he thought. He did appreciate having someone on the same page as him. "And then he said it didn't make any difference to him one way or the other." He sighed in frustration. "How can we change that kind of thinking?"

"It's quite a challenge," Ashley agreed. "I know that Sharpay thinks that offering the students some showbiz razzle-dazzle will do the trick . . . oops!" She covered her mouth as if realizing too late that she was revealing an inside secret. "I guess I shouldn't have said that."

"That's okay, I'll forget I heard anything," Troy promised. "After all, I want to win this election fair and square. . . ."

"—Especially since it's supposed to be a *huge* secret that we're going to sing a special song in the cafeteria today to rally people to our side," Ashley said. She stopped abruptly and bit her lip coyly. "Oops, again!"

"I didn't hear a thing," Troy reassured her, even though his mind was spinning. Sharpay

48

was going to stage a musical number to get people's votes? He should've known she would do something like that. If he didn't come up with something fast, this election was going to be a landslide for the Drama Club!

"Really?" Ashley gave him a melting look. "You'll forget I said anything?"

"My memory has been wiped clean," he said, doing his best to smile even as he tried to think what the basketball team could possibly do to compete with Sharpay.

"Thank you so much! I really wouldn't want to damage Sharpay's campaign in any way!" she said, doe-eyed. "I guess I just got carried away, because I know how much it means to you to get the gym renovated. And even though I would *love* to have nicer dressing rooms in the theater, I also really, really care about *you* being happy—"

"Um, yeah, thanks," Troy said, flustered.

"—And the rest of the basketball team, too, of course," Ashley finished.

Out of the corner of his eye, Troy saw

Gabriella enter the classroom. He jumped to his feet. "Well, thanks so much; glad we could have this little chat; no reason for us to be enemies just because we're on opposite sides," he said quickly. "See you around!"

He had already given her a big politician's smile and a hearty handshake when he suddenly remembered—he wasn't going anywhere, because class was about to start. He blushed as Gabriella walked up to join them.

"Hey, guys," she said, raising one eyebrow. "Glad to see you're showing so much bipartisan spirit."

"What?" Ashley asked, confused.

"That's what it's called when two political parties work together," Gabriella explained. She glanced sideways at Troy. "Except, you're not really working together, right?"

"Oh, um, no," he said. "We're just doing some bipartisan . . . chatting."

"That's what I thought," Gabriella said cheerfully. She totally trusted Troy. As for Ashley, well, she didn't trust her one little bit. As Ashley hurried across the room to take her seat, Gabriella slipped into the desk next to Troy's and leaned over to whisper, "So what did she want, anyway?"

"Nothing much," he said casually. "I think we'd better put our campaign into overdrive, though. If we don't, Sharpay could end up winning this election!"

CHAPTER FIVE

By lunchtime, Troy couldn't wait to sit down, eat his sandwich, and forget all about the election for one brief hour. But as soon as he sat down with Chad, Zeke, and Jason at their usual table, Nathan rushed over, his arms full of several thick binders.

"Hi, guys," he said breathlessly. "Listen, I stayed up until midnight crunching the numbers from my latest poll. The results are fascinating. I discovered some very interesting patterns, especially when I did an analysis comparing the responses according to various demographic groups, such as the different grades. And the gender breakdown was also quite illuminating—"

"Dude, slow down and start over!" Chad laughed. "You lost me somewhere after 'Hi, guys.'"

"Don't worry, I'll go over everything using one-syllable words when I'm done," Nathan said impatiently, as he pushed their lunch trays aside so that he could dump the binders on the table. "Now, see, this is the most crucial bit of information that I extracted from all the raw data—"

But then he was interrupted once again, this time by members of the Drama Club, led by Sharpay, who burst into the cafeteria. They were followed by two dozen band members, who were all playing a catchy, upbeat song.

Sharpay and her campaign team began dancing around the cafeteria, singing loudly and clapping their hands.

"Hey, hey, we want your vote!
For that we'll sing any note,
Because we want a groovy stage,
Now that musicals are all the rage!"

By the end of the first stanza, all the students in the cafeteria were tapping their toes to the music. By the time the singers reached the first chorus, some people were on their feet and dancing. By the big finish, which involved Sharpay and Ryan leaping on top of a table and doing a few high kicks, everyone was cheering and applauding.

The only people who weren't having a great time watching this performance of Sharpay's campaign song were the ones sitting at Troy's table. The mood there was decidedly glum.

"Well, there goes my appetite," Chad said grumpily. He pushed his lunch tray aside.

"Mine too," Zeke said. "And these tacos were really good," he added.

Troy just sat with his arms folded. He wasn't

mad at Sharpay for doing a great job; he was mad at himself for not coming up with anything that could come close to matching it.

"I hate to admit it," he said sheepishly, "but Sharpay's idea was great. She knows how to get people excited about her platform."

"So we just have to figure out how to beat her at her own game," Chad said. "There's no way kids in this school would rather have some fancy theater lights than a cool gym!"

"I'm afraid you're wrong about that." Nathan had barely looked up during the song, ignoring the pandemonium in the cafeteria as he had flipped through the pages of his binders. Now he stared seriously around the table. "As I was saying, support for the gym renovation shows a lot of weakness among non-athletes, who feel that they won't get any benefit from it—"

"But who's going to benefit from fancy dressing rooms?" Zeke pointed out. "The Drama Club, that's who!"

Nathan shook his head in irritatation. "That's

not the point. Sharpay has managed to frame her issue in a way that appeals to everyone. You heard her song: *Now that musicals are all the rage*? Everyone who went to *Twinkle Towne*—which is pretty much every person in this school—is going to think, 'Oh, if I vote for Sharpay, we'll get to see more great shows!'"

The boys sat back and thought about this for a moment. Finally, Chad said, "So, you mean that because our man Troy here starred in that musical and did an awesome job, we're going to end up losing out on an awesome gym?"

"Well, that's not *quite* the spin I would put on it," Nathan said, glancing uneasily at Troy.

Three pairs of eyes suddenly swiveled to glare accusingly at Troy.

"Hey, guys, it doesn't do any good to point fingers," Nathan said hastily.

"Yeah," Troy agreed. "Let's figure out how we can regain some traction in this election—and fast!"

That night, Troy, Chad, Jason, and Zeke joined Taylor and Gabriella at Gabriella's house. Mrs. Montez put out a plate of cookies, a bowl of popcorn, and sodas, and then left them alone.

"Okay, everyone," Troy said. "Sharpay did a great job today. We might as well admit it."

"So the Drama Club sang a song!" Chad protested. "Big deal! That's not going to be enough to get everybody to vote for the auditorium renovation!"

"Sharpay doesn't need *everybody's* vote," Taylor reminded him. "She only needs to get one more vote than we get!"

"Right," Troy agreed. "So what can we do to fight back? We've got to think of a stunt that will get more East High students on our side."

A silence fell over the group. Troy jotted a few ideas on his notepad. Zeke and Jason stared off into space, furrowing their brows in thought. Taylor tapped her pencil thoughtfully on the table. Chad tilted back in his chair and looked at the ceiling, as if the answer might be written there. Gabriella gazed out the window.

Finally, Troy said, "How about this? We could hand out flyers explaining why voting for the gym makes more sense."

There was a long pause. Then Chad said, "Good idea, dude, but it's kind of . . . boring, you know?"

"Yeah," Zeke said. "I mean, the Drama Club sang! They danced! They had people cheering!"

Jason nodded. "A flyer's going to look pretty lame against that."

Gabriella sneaked a quick glance at Troy. He looked downcast at the reception his idea had received. He was frowning down at his legal pad and making some grumpy notations.

"I don't think it's a bad idea," she said loyally. "Sure, everybody got excited about their routine, but once they look at the facts—"

Taylor sighed and shook her head. "That would be great if people voted logically, but they don't," she said. "As a scientist, it pains me to say this, but we won't win the election through facts and figures."

"Right!" Chad chimed in. "We need to come up with a really cool stunt that will be even better than Sharpay's."

Gabriella frowned. Taylor and Chad were right. She knew that, but still . . .

"I'm not sure we should be trying to think of a 'stunt,'" she insisted. "Take a look at this chart that Nathan made." Gabriella picked up the folder of Nathan's reports. He had created a chart that showed, day by day, how the East High students planned to vote.

She pointed out how the votes constantly swung back and forth, depending on which team had just pulled off a big stunt. All that it seemed to show was that East High students were willing to change their vote from one day to the next, depending on who had just grabbed their attention. "So that means that, even if we come up with something great tomorrow, we'll only have people's votes until Sharpay comes up with something better," she finished. "And in the meantime, no one's even paying attention to the real issues."

There was a moment of complete silence in the Montez living room. Then Troy said, "You make a really good point, Gabriella. But I think these guys are right. My idea of creating flyers just won't get the voters excited. Like it or not, we've got to beat Sharpay at her own game!"

CHAPTER SIX

"**H**mm. I wonder what's going on over there?" Sharpay said as she stood with Ryan in the school courtyard the next morning. It was Wednesday, only two and a half days before the election, and Troy's campaign team seemed far too upbeat. She frowned suspiciously at the sight of Troy and his friends laughing and joking around. They looked excited, happy, and very, very confident.

"I don't know," Ryan said, echoing her wary

tone, "but they look like they've got a trick up their sleeve." He glanced at Sharpay. "Should we be worried, sis?"

She lifted one eyebrow with disdain. "Of course not," she snapped. "When it comes to tricks, we can match and beat whatever they have!"

Across the courtyard, Chad noticed how Sharpay was eyeing them. He laughed. "Dude, we've really got Sharpay worried!" he said.

"She should be," Troy replied. "After all, thanks to you guys, we came up with not one, but *two* awesome ideas last night!"

"I can't wait to see their faces at lunchtime," Taylor added gleefully.

But their good spirits didn't last. Nathan came over to deliver some bad news.

Nathan's polls showed that Sharpay's song-and-dance stunt had worked. Support for the auditorium renovation had shot up to thirty-seven percent among students who intended to vote. And, even more impressively, the number of students who were now showing an interest in the election had surged a whopping sixty-three percent. Gabriella and Troy exchanged uneasy glances.

The first bell rang, and they started for homeroom. Nathan walked with them, still flipping obsessively through his papers.

As they went inside, Chad's big smile disappeared. "I can't believe we're losing!" he cried.

"They're not that far ahead. We can still catch up," Troy said, but he looked concerned.

"Don't worry," Gabriella said. "Remember, we've got a great event planned. I'm sure we'll win over a lot of students today."

The others looked reassured. They had stayed up late the night before, calling other friends to get the day's event organized. Today at lunchtime, the plan would swing into action— and if all went as they hoped, they would pull ahead in the polls and stay there until the election.

"Anyway, we haven't lost until the last vote is counted," Taylor pointed out.

"That's right," Troy said. "We've come from behind on the basketball court. We can do it here, too."

Nathan nodded, but he was looking thoughtful. "Statistically, the closer it gets to Election Day, the harder it is to overcome any lead built by the opposing party," he warned. "You only have a couple of days left."

Sharpay had been walking down the hall when she saw her opponents having what seemed to be a serious discussion, so she veered closer. She managed to overhear Nathan's last remark. "What is this I hear?" she asked brightly. "Is Team Basketball getting worried?"

"In your dreams!" Chad shot back. "Our only worry is how we're going to celebrate our victory!"

"But as Nathan said, you only have a few days left," she said sweetly. "And even fewer ideas, I'm sure." She tossed her head and gave Troy a challenging smile. "Are you sure you don't want to concede to me right now? It would really save everyone so much time and trouble."

"Thanks for the offer, Sharpay, but I'm not ready to give in just yet," Troy said, smiling. "Although if you want to concede by the end of the day, feel free to give me a call."

He gave his team a wink, and they all started down the hall to their first class, leaving Sharpay staring after them.

Hmm, she wondered. What was that all about? Troy and his campaign team seemed awfully sure of themselves . . . and that couldn't be a good thing.

By lunchtime, word had spread that Troy's team had planned something big to get support for their campaign, but no one had a clue as to what it was. There was a buzz of anticipation in the cafeteria as students glanced around the room, wondering what was going to happen.

They didn't have long to wait. A few minutes after lunch had started, the cafeteria doors burst open, and the East High cheerleaders bounded into the room. They shook their pom-poms and began to cheer loudly:

"Who always plays to win?
Wildcats! Wildcats!
Who needs a brand-new gym?
Wildcats! Wildcats!
Who are the champions?
Wildcats! Wildcats!
Vote, Wildcats! Vote, Wildcats! Vote, Wildcats!
Yay!"

By the end of the cheer, everyone was standing and clapping along. The cheerleaders did a series of cartwheels across the floor, then jumped into the air, waving their pom-poms. Troy cleared a space in the middle of the room and did a few basket tosses, which had the crowd going wild. The cheerleaders finished by having the audience chant, *"Get out the vote!"*, and getting everyone on their feet. The noise level was several decibels higher than normal when the cheerleaders jogged out of the cafeteria. As students began leaving to go to their next class, several people stopped by Troy's table.

"Man, that was great!" one freshman boy said earnestly. "You've got my vote, for sure!"

"Yeah, I was going to vote for the auditorium," a girl added, "but the pep rally reminded me of how much fun I always have at basketball games."

"And you guys won the championship!" another boy chimed in. "You totally deserve a better place to practice."

Troy and Chad smiled in satisfaction, while Gabriella and Taylor gave each other a high five.

"We can take this election to the bank!" Chad said enthusiastically.

"Having a pep rally was incredible," Troy agreed. "That was a great idea, Taylor."

Before Taylor could answer him, Sharpay came over to their table, a scowl on her face. "Yes, great idea," she said frostily. "Though, of course, it was sadly derivative of what we did. If you want to keep the voters' support, you should try to be a little more original."

"Come on, Sharpay, lighten up!" Chad said in a teasing voice. "No one likes a sore loser."

She raised her eyebrows in disdain. "Really? That's an excellent piece of advice, Chad. You should keep it in mind on Friday—when you *lose*!"

And with that, she stomped away.

At first, Sharpay was so mad at how much everyone had liked the pep rally—and so irritated that her own brilliant idea had been used against her—that she couldn't even think straight. By the time she reached her locker, however, she had cooled down a little bit. She spotted Ashley and Ryan in the hall and motioned for them to join her in the empty choir room.

"Wow, the cheerleaders really got that crowd fired up," Ryan began, his eyes wide. "My ears are still ringing!"

"Yes, yes, yes, their little stunt was quite impressive in its small, small way," Sharpay said impatiently. "And you know what? I'm actually glad."

Ryan and Ashley stared at her with identical openmouthed expressions.

"You're glad that Troy might win?" Ashley gasped.

"Of course not!" Sharpay snapped. "I'm glad that they're finally offering us some competition. After all, it would have been hard to keep up the excitement all by ourselves. And this will spur us on and make us even more determined to win!"

Ryan nodded, filled with admiration for his sister. "You're right. Tonight's rehearsal should be great, now that we know exactly what we're up against."

"*Ye-e-ss,*" Sharpay said. "But I was thinking more about using our newfound determination in a slightly more, um, *political* way."

Ryan and Ashley exchanged confused glances.

"I thought we *were* doing things in a political way," Ashley said. "I mean, we've been painting posters and staging events and talking constantly to anyone who will listen to us about how important the auditorium renovation is—"

"Mmm, well, perhaps *political* wasn't quite the right word," Sharpay said. "I guess what I really meant was that we should start doing things in a slightly more, well . . ." She waved one hand in the air as if reaching for the word she wanted.

But Sharpay didn't have to reach far. Ryan recognized the expression on his sister's face, and he helpfully supplied the right word for her. "A slightly more *sneaky* way?" he offered.

Sharpay smiled smugly at him. "Exactly," she said. "So, Ashley, I've noticed that you've been very friendly with Troy lately. . . ."

Ashley's heart skipped a beat. Was Sharpay mad at her for talking to the competition? Even worse, did she suspect that Ashley was giving Troy little hints to help him win the election?

"I think that's a very good approach," Sharpay went on. Ashley breathed a sigh of relief. "Keep talking to him, acting nice and cozy. He'll let his

THE CAMPAIGN TRAIL

Whether it is being popular, winning the lead in the latest musical **(BARRING ONE NOTABLE FREAK EXCEPTION!)**, or setting fashion trends, I aim to be number one. It is no different on the campaign trail. In fact, since there is a vote to determine an actual winner, I find that it really flames my competitive spirit. After all, no one runs a campaign race hoping to be runner-up. Even poor deluded Troy and all his sweaty cronies campaigned against me trying to claim the victory. Unfortunately they forgot one little thing: I do most things really well, but **WINNING IS WHAT I DO BEST!**

SHARPAY AND RYAN'S 'HOW TO' GUIDE

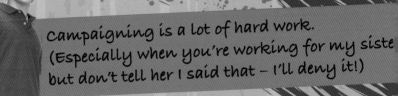

Campaigning is a lot of hard work. (Especially when you're working for my siste but don't tell her I said that – I'll deny it!)

We would never want to give away all of our campaign secrets, but here are a few things to remember if you need to campaign for something.

1 Don't campaign against us. You will lose. Badly. We are serious.

2 Being a figurehead on a campaign means you will constantly be on display. There is not time for a 'bad hair day' or splotchy skin. You should always look your best, but this is especially true when campaigning. So spend a little more prep time in front of the mirror.

3 Anything you say can further your campaign (or damage it!). Pick and choose your words with extra care. People usually think of themselves first (and with good reason!) so anytime you are speaking to someone whose vote you want to influence, try to think of what it is they want. You need to convince them that what they want and what you want are the same thing or will at least complement each other.

4 Unfortunately, you can't just talk to people that you normally associate with. No doubt, they already like you and their votes are secure. You will need to force yourself to talk to groups you wouldn't normally even dream of being seen with. Stinky athletes, boring brainiacs, shiftless skateboarders, etc. It's unpleasant, but just remind yourself that it's for a larger cause: your victory!

TROY AND GABRIELLA'S GUIDE TO RAISING AWARENESS

I thought basketball practice was tough, but getting people interested in what you are campaigning about can be a lot of hard work!

But if it's a cause you believe in, it will all be worth it in the end. With the in mind, here are a few top tips for raising awareness.

1 **Be honest. This should go without saying, but you should never run a sneaky or dishonest campaign. People almost always find out in the end, and then you will not only lose votes (and probably the campaign) but more importantly, you will lose people's trust and respect.**

2 Pick a cause you believe in. If you're just doing it to impress people or be popular, or even just for the sake of winning, you're doing it for the wrong reasons. If it's something you really believe in, people will respond to your sincerity.

3 Sometimes you need to think outside the box in order to really get people interested. Consider alternative ways to get people's attention. Try hosting a picnic/rally. People will come for the free food, and then you can try to win them over. Or challenge your opponent to a public debate.

4 If it's something that you truly believe in, you should try to raise awareness about the topic even if you aren't running an official campaign. There is no time like the present, so get started now!

HOW HOT IS YOUR CAMPAIGN?

Take this test to find out if you're a cool campaigner or a lazy loser.

1. What is the best part of campaigning?

A. TRYING TO MAKE A DIFFERENCE OR POSITIVE CHANGE

B. THE COMPETITION

C. TALKING TO EVERYBODY. I LOVE TALKING AND THIS IS A REALLY GOOD EXCUSE!

D. SOMETIMES TEACHERS WILL LET YOU OUT OF CLASS TO 'CAMPAIGN'

2. What is the worst part of campaigning?

A. FAILING TO CHANGE PEOPLE'S MINDS OR HEARTS

B. LOSING

C. WHEN THE EXCITEMENT OF THE CAMPAIGN IS OVER

D. UH. CAMPAIGNING. PROBABLY – IT'S A LOT OF WORK!

3. You are debating an opponent and he challenges you with a question you don't really have a good answer for – how do you respond?

A. I THANK HIM/HER FOR RAISING AN IMPORTANT ISSUE AND I TRY TO DISCUSS HOW IT IS A COMPLEX MATTER

B. I GLARE AT MY OPPONENT BEFORE RIDICULING HIM/HER FOR TRYING TO STEER THE DEBATE AWAY FROM REALLY IMPORTANT MATTERS

C. I SHRUG MY SHOULDERS AND LAUGH

D. I DON'T PLAN ON DOING A LOT OF PREPARATION. SO I IMAGINE I'LL GET A LOT OF THOSE QUESTIONS

4. You discover that your opponent has been telling lies about you in order to ruin your campaign – what do you do?

A. WATER PUTS OUT FIRES AND HONESTY PUTS OUT DISHONESTY – I HOLD AN OPEN FORUM TO SET THE RECORD STRAIGHT

B. I ESCALATE THE BATTLE BY TELLING EVEN MORE HORRENDOUS LIES ABOUT MY OPPONENT

C. I WOULD APPROACH MY OPPONENT PRIVATELY AND ASK THEM TO CLEAR THE AIR

D. THAT'S POLITICS, BABY!

5. You find out that some of your team has been loafing instead of doing work on the campaign – how do you respond?

A. I TALK TO THEM INDIVIDUALLY AND TRY TO CONVINCE THEM HOW IMPORTANT THEIR JOBS ARE AND HOW SERIOUS THE CAMPAIGN IS

B. I FIRE THEM IMMEDIATELY AND HIRE RESPONSIBLE HELP!

C. I MIGHT TRY TO SET A BETTER EXAMPLE. OR I MIGHT JUST JOIN THEM – DEPENDS ON MY MOOD AT THE TIME

D. WHO CAN BLAME THEM REALLY?

6. How will you handle it if you lose the campaign?

A. IT WILL JUST INSPIRE ME TO TRY HARDER NEXT TIME

B. I MIGHT CRY. I MIGHT SCREAM. I MIGHT PRETEND TO BE ILL FOR A COUPLE OF DAYS – I HATE LOSING

C. WIN SOME. LOSE SOME – NOT A BIG DEAL EITHER WAY

D. I'M JUST DOING IT FOR THE ATTENTION REALLY – I DON'T CARE ABOUT THE WINNING OR LOSING

ANSWER KEY:

If you answered mostly **A**s, you are extremely dedicated to the campaign and your cause — your chances of winning are good and you might have a future in politics.

If you answered mostly **B**s, you are a political animal, but the problem is you're too focused on winning rather than your cause. Try to lighten up, get back to what you want to achieve after winning, and have fun as well.

If you answered mostly **C**s, you know how to have fun, but the problem is you might be having too much fun — try to remember that anything worth doing is worth doing well.

If you answered mostly **D**s, your chances of winning are exceptionally poor — politics just really isn't your thing.

guard down. That's when you can sneak in a question or two about what they have planned."

Ashley had to work hard to suppress a grin. Sharpay was actually encouraging her to get close to Troy? She couldn't have planned this better herself! She nodded slowly, as if very impressed with Sharpay's reasoning. "That's a great idea, Sharpay," she said sweetly. "I'll be sure to get on that right away."

CHAPTER SEVEN

The next morning, Nathan asked the members of both campaigns to meet him in the courtyard before homeroom. He had decided to start doing bipartisan briefings, both to avoid accusations of favoritism and to reduce his stress levels.

The closer it got to the election, the more both campaign teams had been peppering him with questions and trying to find out what their opponents were doing. He was beginning to think wistfully of how nice and quiet life had been when all he had had to think about was whether to spend an extra hour on his history homework or his science-fair project.

On the plus side, he had now definitely ruled out politics as a future career choice, a decision which would, of course, seriously damage the democratic process in the future—but it was the present he had to worry about.

And right now, the democratic process was already looking pretty bad.

"So, Nathan," Troy asked. "How'd we do?"

Nathan cleared his throat. "Well, it seems the pep rally was very effective. By a very slight margin—33 to 30 percent—more students are now planning on voting for the gym."

"Those numbers can't be right!" Sharpay yelled. "The batteries in that little calculator you carry everywhere must be dead!"

He stepped away from her with as much dignity as he could muster. "I assure you, my calculations are always correct," he said coldly.

"Yes!" Chad pumped a fist into the air. "The new gym is ours!"

Nathan's eyes narrowed in displeasure. "I wouldn't get too carried away," he said. "My poll indicates that 37 percent of the student body is still undecided, which is a significant percentage. It's still a wide-open race."

"Ha!" Sharpay cried triumphantly, her arms folded across her chest. "And we have something very special planned for today!" She arched one eyebrow as she added, "What about you, Troy? Do you have anything to follow up your little pep rally?"

"Of course," he said, trying to sound confident.

Nathan shot him a curious look. He'd been hanging out with Troy and his friends quite a bit over the last few days, and he hadn't heard any ideas other than the pep rally.

Oh, well, he thought. It wasn't his business. All he had to do was conduct his polls and run his numbers. What the politicians did with his data was up to them.

"So, that's it until tomorrow," he said, briskly snapping his briefcase shut. "I'll do another poll this afternoon. Until then, good luck to you all."

"Sharpay seems very sure of herself," Troy commented as he walked with Gabriella to homeroom.

"I know," she replied. "I wonder what she has planned?"

They didn't have to wait long to find out. When homeroom ended, everyone went to their lockers to get books for their first class. As students hurried through the halls, they were confronted with . . . drama! It was happening around every corner!

The students heading toward the north staircase found Ryan and Alicia doing a scene from *Up the Down Staircase* on the landing. The students who rushed to PE class found Sharpay, Charlotte, and several other Drama Club members acting out a scene from *A Midsummer Night's Dream* in the gym.

All day long, as students hurried through the halls, they found themselves running into Drama Club members doing Hamlet's soliloquy in front of the guidance counselor's office, or singing a song from *Guys and Dolls* inside the language lab, or acting out a scene from *Little Shop of Horrors* near the band room.

By lunchtime, the whole school was buzzing with talk of the election.

Sharpay got to her next class late, still flushed with excitement after having received a loud round of applause in the north corridor. She saw Troy and gave him a triumphant wave. "That's the power of theater!" she boasted, taking her seat. "Now everyone at East High knows what they'll get when they vote for me—stunning, dramatic performances in a state-of-the-art auditorium that they will remember for the rest of their lives!"

"Actually, no one will be voting for you," said Nathan, turning around from his seat in the front row.

She frowned at him. "*Excuse* me?"

"They will be voting for the auditorium renovation," he explained in his know-it-all way. "Not for you, per se. For the auditorium."

"Oh, well, what*ever*," she said, tossing her blonde hair. "The point is, I am well on the way to victory." She smirked at Troy. "Care to go ahead and admit defeat?"

"No way," Troy said, shaking his head. He felt his competitive spirit kick into high gear at the very thought of conceding. "You wait, Sharpay. This campaign isn't over yet!"

Troy was more worried than he let on, however. He asked permission from the lunchroom monitor to be excused from lunch so he could go to the library instead. He needed some peace and quiet to work on the final details of their next campaign surprise, which was happening immediately after school.

He waved to Miss Falstaff, the librarian, who looked lonely. Usually, most of the tables were filled with students working on research papers or studying for tests. Today, however, everyone was too excited about the drama that was spreading through the halls to spend any time studying.

That's even better, Troy thought. Now I can really concentrate, with no one here to disturb me.

He sat down at a table and spread out all of his papers. He had a folder with all of Nathan's reports, as well as pages of notes that he had taken after every discussion with the members of his election campaign.

More importantly, he had the list he had started the night before, when they had all planned their second big surprise event. It was a great idea, one that he felt sure would win them the election.

Cheered by this thought, he started reviewing his notes. After twenty minutes, he sighed and leaned back in his chair, closing his eyes. This election stuff is a lot harder than I expected, he thought.

"Having a hard time with the election?" a voice said next to his ear. "Or are you actually doing homework?"

Troy jumped and opened his eyes to see Ashley standing over him. She was smiling sympathetically.

"Sorry." She kept smiling. "I didn't mean to disturb you."

"That's okay," Troy said. He spotted the books she was carrying and raised his eyebrows in surprise. "What are you doing here, anyway? I thought you'd be acting in some of the scenes that Sharpay's been staging all over the school."

She shook her head. "I did a few scenes this morning, but I told Sharpay that I couldn't participate this afternoon. I have a major geometry test coming up, and I'm terrible at geometry! I got permission to come to the library during my lunch break so I could study."

"Oh." Troy was rather impressed. After the way Ashley had schemed her way into getting an invitation to Sharpay's birthday party, well, he had written her off as another one of Sharpay's toadies. But it looked as if Ashley might actually have a mind of her own. "Well, good for you. It takes discipline to focus on your studies—and it takes real guts to say no to Sharpay!"

Ashley laughed. "Thanks, Troy." She started to pull a chair out from the table, then hesitated. "Oh . . . is it all right if I join you? I'll be as quiet as a mouse, I promise!"

"Sure," Troy said. "And it's not like you'd be interrupting any deep thoughts on my part. I'm just making a list of things we need to do. . . ."

Just in time, he remembered: Ashley was working for the opposition! She might have stood up to Sharpay when it came to studying, but she still wanted Sharpay's campaign to end up victorious. He closed his mouth with a snap.

"If you want to bounce some ideas off me, go ahead," Ashley offered, her voice dripping with sweetness.

"Thanks, but I think I've got this wrapped up," Troy said politely.

"Oh, okay." She examined her fingernails and added casually, "So, how are you feeling about the election? You know, since everyone votes tomorrow . . ."

"Good," Troy said immediately. "Good, good, good. Excellent, in fact."

Ashley tilted her head to one side and smiled at him. "Don't worry, I won't breathe a word of what you say to anybody else—not even Sharpay. After all, we're sitting here as friends, right? And if you said something to me because I'm your friend and then I turned around and used that against you . . . well, that would be unethical, wouldn't it?"

Troy hesitated.

Ashley looked hurt. "Don't you trust me, Troy?"

"No, no, it's not that," he said quickly. "It's just—"

How could he say that he was afraid to tell her anything in case it gave Sharpay an edge?

At that moment, rescue came from an unlikely source.

"Troy, excuse me." Miss Falstaff was standing beside their table, looking anxious. "I think I left my keys in the teachers' lounge, and I can't rest easy until I go find them. Would you mind answering the phone for me until I get back? It will only take five minutes, and it's very quiet today. . . ."

"Of course," he said immediately. He got up and started to head to the librarian's office, then glanced back at his books. They were spread in a heap all over the table.

Ashley seemed to read his mind. "Don't worry," she said sweetly. "I'll be here until the end of the lunch period trying to figure out this geometry! I'll watch your stuff until you get back."

"Thanks," Troy replied. He hurried off.

He didn't see Ashley staring thoughtfully after him, or taking a peek inside his notebook.

CHAPTER EIGHT

After Troy finished reviewing his campaign strategy in the library, he headed to his locker to grab his books. He ran into Nathan, Chad, Gabriella, and Taylor in the hallway.

"Troy!" Nathan called out. "Glad I caught you."

"What is it, Statistics Man?" Chad taunted. "Let me guess. You've been running some more numbers, right?"

Taylor shushed Chad, but Nathan wasn't

paying attention to the teasing. He looked at Troy with his usual intense, unblinking stare and said, "Troy, I have good news and bad news. Which do you want to hear first?"

This was a no-brainer, as far as Troy was concerned. "Let me hear the bad news," he said, bracing himself.

Nathan was holding his binder, which was even thicker than it had been the day before. He flipped it open and pointed to one particular page. "Okay. The bad news is that the dramatic readings Sharpay staged earlier today were very effective. The support for the auditorium renovation jumped twelve points."

Chad groaned and leaned his head back against the lockers. "That figures. After all, who can resist a good soliloquy?"

"Wait, what does a twelve-point jump mean?" Taylor asked. "Are we still ahead, or have we fallen behind in the polls?"

"Excellent question." Nathan gave a crisp nod of approval. "With twelve more points, Sharpay's team has moved ahead. They are winning by nine points."

"Nine points?" Chad cried. "It's the day before the election! At this point, we should be dominating!"

"Don't worry," Troy said. "Today's our last push! The polls open at two p.m. tomorrow, and all anyone's going to be talking about is our last big surprise!"

But Taylor shook her head. "Yeah, but who knows what else Sharpay has planned? You know she's not going to stop now that the tide is turning her way."

Nathan had snapped his binder shut and was checking his text messages as they talked, but this caught his attention. "Well, there are still undecideds out there. And you do have . . ."—he checked his watch—"tomorrow until two p.m. to get them on your side. So, best of luck to you. I'm off to give my report to Sharpay now. I'll see you guys later."

"What?" Chad was outraged. "You're going

to tell her everything you just told us?"

Nathan gave Chad a cool stare. "Of course," he replied. "I told you before; I'm a neutral participant in this election. I don't support one side more than the other. In fact, if it were up to me, the school-board money wouldn't be used for either the gym *or* the auditorium. After all, some students don't really use either facility very often."

Gabriella looked over at Troy. Would he remember that this had been the very point she had made when the entire issue of renovating the school first came up?

"What would you use the money for, Nathan?" Gabriella asked.

"Updating the computer lab, of course," he answered, clearly annoyed.

"Of course," Chad said. "There's a cause that will get everyone really excited."

"I realize that only the most academically gifted students care about such things," Nathan said stiffly. "But if I couldn't have a new computer lab, I guess I'd want . . ." He stopped in midsentence, looking embarrassed.

"What?" Taylor asked. She was genuinely curious about what might have interested Nathan other than computers, advanced placement courses, and acing every test he took.

Nathan shuffled his feet, then said, "Well, it's frivolous, I know. But it would be great to have a place to buy snacks in the afternoon after the cafeteria closes. Not junk, of course," he added hastily. "I'm talking protein-rich brain food that would give every student the energy needed to study for that one extra hour that could make the difference between an A and an A plus!"

Chad rolled his eyes. All he wanted from a snack was something that kept his stomach from growling in Ms. Barrington's fifth-period English class.

Troy smiled. "Well, today might be your lucky day, Nathan! Meet us in the courtyard right after school, and let's see what we can do about hooking you up with a snack. Although, it might not be *that* healthy," Troy said with a wink.

"Step right up, folks, and hear all the reasons why you should vote for the gym!" Zeke called out, grinning. "And by the way, enjoy a delicious treat at the same time!"

The final school bell of the day had just rung. Most of the students headed outside, gathering to chat with their friends in the courtyard.

Zeke was standing behind a table piled high with cupcakes shaped like basketballs. A sign on the table read, VOTE FOR THE GYM! VICTORY IS SWEET! Chad and Taylor were handing out cupcakes as fast as they could while Troy chatted with the students who had clustered around, giving a speech about why they should vote for the gym. Gabriella stood with Zeke and helped put out more cupcakes when the ones on the table were gone.

"This is a great idea, Gabriella!" Taylor brushed a strand of hair away from her forehead and helped her open another box filled with cupcakes.

"Well, everyone likes dessert," Gabriella said.

"*Especially* when it's a pastry," Zeke added. Zeke loved sweets more than anything.

"Stop acting modest, Gabriella," Chad said. "You're a political mastermind!"

Taylor nodded. "When I run for president, I want you at my side."

Everyone laughed. They had found out that Taylor harbored lofty political ambitions the previous Halloween, when they all had to dress as their future selves for an East High costume party. Taylor's declarations, which always started with "When I run for president . . ." had become a running joke.

Gabriella glanced down to hide how pleased she was at the compliment. "Thanks, but Zeke's the real hero," she said. "After all, if he didn't know how to make awesome cupcakes, we would have been completely out of luck."

Troy overheard her remark and stopped

greeting the voters long enough to say, "You were the one who created the basketball cupcake, though, Gabriella." He gave her a warm smile. "That was a Valentine's Day gift I'll never forget."

She blushed, but before she could reply, Sharpay and Ryan walked over. They couldn't even get close to the table because of the crowd, but Sharpay's eyes flashed as she saw dozens of students happily eating cupcakes. Ryan frowned as he heard Chad say to a small group gathered around him, "And if we win the election, we'll get a flashy, new high-tech scoreboard!"

"Cool!" one of the kids exclaimed as he licked the last few crumbs from his cupcake wrapper.

Chad nodded enthusiastically. "It'll flash slogans that people can chant!" he promised. "It'll show instant replays from the game!"

"Awesome!" one of the other kids said. "Hey, can I have another cupcake?"

"Sure!" Chad said, handing one over with an expansive gesture. "In fact, you can have two."

He grabbed another cupcake and gave it to the hungry student.

Finally, the crowd thinned enough for Sharpay to edge her way to the table. There were only crumbs left.

"What an interesting idea," she said slowly. "Using food to woo the voters."

"Interesting? Brilliant, you mean!" Chad gave her a cocky grin. "Aren't you sorry you didn't think of it?"

Sharpay had a funny little smile on her face.

What's she up to? Troy thought. She didn't look as upset as he would have expected.

She didn't even react when one student said to another, "You know, I wasn't going to vote for the gym, but I've changed my mind. These cupcakes are amazing!"

"I can't believe it!" Everyone turned to look at Nathan, who had just joined them. He had been canvassing the crowd and now stood before them, his clipboard in hand and his eyes running over the numbers he had scribbled down. "I haven't had time to do a more precise analysis, of course, but my initial data indicates that the gym issue is now ahead. I just don't understand it."

"What's to understand?" Troy asked, feeling a little smug. "Gabriella had a great idea, Zeke had a great recipe, and the rest, as they say, is just history."

Chad high-fived him, but Nathan was shaking his head slowly, looking extremely disapproving. "The reasons people are giving for their decision are so irrational! In fact, seventy-eight percent of the gym voters say they're voting for the gym because they like cupcakes! *Cupcakes!*" He gave them all a baffled look. "Although I *do* appreciate the after-school snack," he added.

"Speaking of cupcakes . . ." Zeke said as he reached into the pastry box. He pulled out one last cupcake. He held it out to Sharpay with an adoring look on his face. "I know we're on the opposite side and everything, but I would love for you to get to taste one of these delicious treats."

"Thank you," she said with a knowing smirk. "But no. I have a feeling there might be something even better coming along."

As if on cue, they suddenly heard the tinny sound of music in the distance. Gradually, it got closer and louder. The group wondered what was going to happen next. Troy and Gabriella exchanged uneasy glances. They looked up to see a fleet of ice-cream trucks coming around the corner and pulling up in front of the courtyard.

Sharpay ran up to the first truck, reached inside the cab to grab a microphone, and struck a pose in front of the East High students who had quickly gathered around.

"Hello, East High!" she yelled. "My name is Sharpay Evans, and I want your vote! Step right up to get your free ice-cream cone and to find out why you should vote to have our auditorium renovated so that it's worthy of my talents!"

Everyone cheered and surged past her to the curb, where people who worked for Sharpay's father served up one ice-cream cone after another.

Troy, Chad, and Gabriella quietly hung back, watching the frenzied scene with dismay.

"I can't believe it!" Chad cried, shaking his head. "She stole our idea!"

"Yeah," Troy said slowly. "And she timed the ice-cream trucks to steal our thunder, too."

"But how could she know we were going to hand out free cupcakes today?" Gabriella wondered. "We all promised to keep it a secret."

A scene flashed through Troy's mind: the library, Ashley, his notebook left behind as he went off to do a good deed . . .

Suddenly, he realized he had fallen into a trap.

"I think this is my fault," he said finally. "Wow. Sharpay works fast," he said, shaking his head.

Gabriella and Chad turned to stare at him.

"What do you mean?" Gabriella asked. She tried to keep her voice calm, but it wasn't easy. She had a sneaking suspicion that Ashley was behind this in some way, and she wasn't sure she wanted to know how.

He quickly explained what he thought had happened. "Of course, I can't prove anything," he said, trying to be fair. "But it seems like an awfully big coincidence—"

"Dude, she totally spied on us to help Sharpay!" Chad exclaimed. He glared across the courtyard. Sharpay was chatting vivaciously with a half-dozen students who were standing around, eating ice cream, and nodding in agreement with everything she said. "I think we should have it out with Sharpay right now!"

"Wait a second," Gabriella interrupted. "Troy's right. We can't accuse Ashley of doing anything wrong. And even if she *did* sneak a peek at Troy's notebook, we don't know that Sharpay asked her to. She could have been working on her own. You know, like a, a . . ." Gabriella tried to think of what a real political insider would call someone like Ashley. "A *rogue operator.*"

She looked so pleased with herself for coming up with the phrase that Troy grinned. Immediately, he felt his mood lift. Gabriella was so calm and reasonable, he thought. It was one of her best qualities—and it was really helpful in the middle of a hard-fought election campaign.

"You're right," he agreed. "And there *is* an upside to this."

"Okay, Mr. Positive, what's that?" Chad asked. He knew from playing basketball that it was important to stay strong and confident in order to win, but he also believed in facing facts. They had been able to hand out maybe a hundred cupcakes. Sharpay had three ice-cream trucks. It looked as if every kid in East High was enjoying an ice-cream cone.

Before Troy could answer, a gaggle of freshman girls walked past. "Mmm, I love butter pecan," one said. "I'm definitely voting for the auditorium. If Sharpay can pull this off, think what she'll do to fix up the theater!"

"I still think it would be better to spend the

money on the gym," another girl argued. "Remember, there are dozens of events held there every month. The auditorium is only used a couple of times a week."

A third girl added, "You know, at first, I wasn't going to vote at all. But now, everyone's talking about this election, and I'm getting kind of interested. And it *is* pretty cool that the school board is letting us decide. . . ."

As they walked away, Troy said, "*That's* the upside, Chad. So what if Sharpay outmaneuvered us? At least we got everybody thinking about the election and excited about voting. And that's what we wanted, right?"

"No, I thought we wanted to win," Chad grumbled, but he looked thoughtful.

Gabriella beamed at Troy. That was a great attitude to take, she thought. That's why he's such a good leader.

They were about to head to class when Sharpay sauntered up with a satisfied grin on her face. The ice-cream trucks had just pulled out of the school parking lot.

"So, what do you think, Troy? Pretty amazing, huh?" she asked, a teasing note in her voice.

"Yeah, Sharpay, it was pretty amazing," he agreed. "In fact, it was great. I think we'll have a great turnout when the polls open tomorrow."

He had to bite his lip to keep from laughing at the look of astonishment on her face. He couldn't help adding, "Although, of course, *your* free ice-cream cones were sadly derivative of *our* free cupcakes. You should really try to be a little more original, don't you think?"

"Hmmph!" Sharpay flipped her hair and stormed away.

Troy, Chad, and Gabriella exchanged glances. Then they all burst out laughing.

CHAPTER NINE

It was Friday, the day of the election. Out of the corner of his eye, Troy noticed Nathan running up to him as he was talking to Gabriella, Chad, Taylor, Jason, and Zeke before school started. Troy knew Nathan took his job seriously, but he wasn't sure he wanted to hear any more statistics or analysis. After all, the voting would start at two o'clock, so there wasn't much he could do if they had fallen behind.

Unfortunately, Nathan had bad news to deliver.

"When it comes to sweet treats," he said, a serious expression on his face, "it's official. East High students prefer ice cream to cupcakes, two to one."

"What?" Zeke was outraged. "Cupcakes are pastries, lovingly stirred together, tenderly baked, and iced to perfection! Ice cream is just . . . frozen milk!"

Nathan shrugged. "Nevertheless, my polls don't lie. Your campaign has fallen behind, and you only have a few hours until the election." He looked at Troy and seemed genuinely sorry. He added, "All I can say now is . . . good luck."

He dashed off again.

"He's probably going to tell Sharpay the good news," Chad muttered. "Man, I don't even want to think about how she'll rub it in if she wins."

"She probably will be pretty obnoxious," Gabriella agreed.

"She's already unbearable! If she actually wins the election—" Taylor shuddered "—she'll be obnoxious to the tenth power!"

"That scoreboard would have been so cool," Jason said mournfully.

"And the banners," Zeke said with a sigh. "Don't forget the banners."

"Come on, guys, we can't give up now!" Gabriella exclaimed. "Remember, Troy gets to give a speech before the vote."

Principal Matsui had decided that Troy and Sharpay could each give a three-minute speech in front of the voters one last time.

"That's true," Chad said. "And if anyone can convince people that renovating the gym is a good thing, it's you, Troy."

"Thanks, but it's not all up to me," Troy said. "We're a team, right? So what if we're trailing by a few points! We still have time for a last-minute push. Let's all divide up and talk to as many people as we can until two o'clock. With all five of us working the halls, we should be able to reach a lot of voters. Are you guys with me?"

"You bet!" Taylor said, her eyes sparkling. "I'll get to every person in my chem lab. And I have a

National Honor Society meeting right before lunch. I'll talk to them, too."

"I've got the south hall covered," Chad volunteered. "And I'll swing through the courtyard during my free period."

By the time each member of the team had come with an action plan, everyone was feeling much better.

"Who's going to win?" Chad yelled.

"We are!" they all yelled back. Then they hurried off to do some last-minute campaigning.

Later that day, Troy stood nervously behind a podium on the auditorium stage, shuffling the notes for his speech in his hands. He was used to being the center of attention on the basketball court. In fact, he was usually so in the zone he didn't even pay attention to the crowd. And when he was onstage, singing with Gabriella—well, he was with Gabriella. That made everything okay.

But now, he could hear the whispers of an auditorium filled with East High students, waiting for his last campaign speech. A bead of sweat rolled down his forehead. The lights seemed abnormally bright and hot. There was such an air of expectancy that his hands even shook a little. He put his notes down on the podium to try to hide it.

But Sharpay, who was standing at another podium a few feet away, had already seen that he was jumpy. She gave him a knowing glance.

Then Principal Matsui took the microphone at the side of the stage. As usual when he touched any sort of audio equipment, it emitted a loud shriek of feedback.

In the audience, Eugene winced.

Finally, Principal Matsui got the microphone under control. "Good afternoon, East High students! As you know, in a few minutes, you will begin voting on how our renovation money will be used. I would like to thank Troy Bolton and Sharpay Evans for running impressive and innovative campaigns. And I would like to thank all of you for the interest and enthusiasm that you have shown over this week for the election. Voting is a right and a privilege. I'm very encouraged to see so many young people who realize they can change their future by using their vote."

The auditorium erupted in applause. Gabriella looked over at Taylor and Chad and gave them a quick grin. Principal Matsui was right—no matter what happened today, they had done something important.

The principal went on, "Now I'd like to invite Sharpay Evans to talk about why she thinks the auditorium and theater should be renovated. Sharpay?"

Sharpay tossed her head and directed a beaming smile around the auditorium. "Thank you, Principal Matsui! I have several reasons for why the auditorium should be renovated. One: We have an incredibly talented group of people in the Drama Club! Their hard work and dedication to theater should be rewarded! Two: Studies show that pleasant, well-kept surroundings can nourish the creative spirit. Think of how much better our productions will be if we have nicer dressing rooms and, perhaps, a new stage curtain. Three: Hel-lo? Primo musicals, anybody? You know we have the best shows in the state, if not the country! Yet other high schools have much better theaters and better equipment! Should East High lag behind? I say no! So, vote for the auditorium and keep theater alive!"

A burst of applause led by Ryan greeted this speech.

Oh, boy, Troy thought. Sharpay sure knows how to work a crowd. He'd realy have to pump up the Wildcat spirit to get people excited about the gym renovation after that!

Before Troy knew it, Principal Matsui was saying, "And now, Troy Bolton, to talk about why the gym should get your vote."

Troy nervously launched into his speech. "Well, um, I guess you guys all know that East High won the district basketball championship," he began.

"Woo-hoo!" someone yelled. It sounded like Chad.

The crowd clapped and cheered enthusiastically. Troy heard a Wildcat howl over the sound of applause. That was *definitely* Chad.

"Yeah, so, that was great. But we don't have anything in the gym to show that we've got a top-notch sports program. Our scoreboard is missing a few bulbs. The walls haven't been painted for years. We don't even have any signs to celebrate our victories."

He heard Sharpay sigh loudly into her microphone and felt a flash of irritation. He had let her speak uninterrupted; at least she could have done the same for him. He plowed on. "And I don't know whether people really know this, but the floorboards are in pretty bad shape. There's one board that kind of sticks up, and it's really easy to trip on. . . ."

The auditorium was so silent that he was sure he could hear someone snoring. He began to sweat. This wasn't going well. His reasons for renovating the gym were good reasons, but they weren't exciting.

In desperation, he threw out the first idea he could think of that might excite the crowd.

"Plus, the games are kind of long, and I know that our fans get hungry," he said. "So I would also propose building a concession stand, so people can get snacks at the game—"

"Wait, wait, wait!" Sharpay interrupted loudly. "What's this about a concession stand? You never mentioned that in your campaign material!"

That's because the idea just came to me, Troy thought. But he knew better than to tell Sharpay that!

"It's a good idea, isn't it?" he asked the crowd.

"Yeah!" they yelled back.

"Well, I want a concession stand, too!" Sharpay yelled. She turned to glare at Troy. "In fact, I distinctly remember thinking of that last week! You stole my idea!"

What am I now—a mind reader? Troy thought. In a deadly accurate impersonation of a politician, he said, "Sharpay, I think that if you examine my previous position statements, you'll find that I have always supported concession stands at East High."

The crowd laughed. They loved the joke—and they loved to see Troy take Sharpay on.

Principal Matsui tapped his watch to indicate that Troy's time was up.

Troy nodded, then leaned into his microphone. "One more thing!" he shouted. "Go, Wildcats!"

Troy had left everyone cheering. He was relieved his speech had gone over well.

Chad gave Troy a high five when he spotted him in the hall after the speeches. "That was awesome," he said. "Where's the victory party going to be?"

"Let's not get too carried away," Gabriella said cautiously. She still gave Troy a quick hug.

At two o'clock, the polls opened. Electronic voting booths were set up in the halls of East High. For the next hour, students lined up to cast their vote. The computer club had created vote-tabulation software that allowed the results to be displayed on an electronic screen in real time. Voting results are never shown in real time in official elections, but Principal Matsui wanted to stress the fact that every vote counted. After people voted, they hung around to watch the vote tally change, minute by minute, as their friends entered the booths and recorded their electronic votes.

Troy was greeted with cheers as he stepped into the voting booth. When he stepped out, there was a roar as the tally changed to 534 votes for the gym and 533 votes for the auditorium.

He grinned and raised his hands over his head. "Here's to a new gym!" Troy cheered.

Then Sharpay and Ryan voted, followed quickly by Ashley, Alicia, and Charlotte. Immediately the tally changed again. It was 538 votes for the auditorium and 534 votes for the gym.

"Ha!" Sharpay tossed her long, blonde hair over her shoulder and smirked at Troy.

The vote count continued to go back and forth. More and more people gathered to watch the electronic tally board shift with every vote.

"Amazing," Taylor commented to Gabriella. "I'm adding up the totals in my head, and I think just about every student will end up voting!"

"Just think—five days ago, people didn't even care about the election!" Gabriella exclaimed. "No matter what happens, this turnout is a victory for everybody."

Chad overheard this. "I agree with you, Gabriella, but I'd still really like to see the gym renovation win—"

At that moment, the tally board changed again. It was 732 for the auditorium, 734 for the gym.

Chad did a little dance. "Yes!"

Principal Matsui stepped in front of the crowd with a megaphone. "The polls are closing in two minutes," he announced. "Two-minute warning."

A few more students hurried into the voting booths, and the tally board changed again. Now the tally was 735 for the auditorium and 734 for the gym.

Troy's shoulders slumped.

Chad's face fell.

Sharpay swept forward and grabbed the megaphone from Principal Matsui's hands. She smiled at the crowd. "I'd like to thank every student at East High for this incredible honor—"

"Wait!" Nathan came running up, his glasses askew on his nose. "I can't believe it! After all that work!" he cried. "I almost forgot to vote!"

Sharpay narrowed her eyes. "But I thought you weren't taking sides!" she exclaimed.

Nathan stiffened. "As a professional, I did my job in an objective manner," he said. "But as a citizen, I get to make my voice heard."

He darted into a voting booth. After a few moments, he exited the booth with a triumphant smile on his face.

A few seconds later, the results board changed.

The score was now 735 to 735.

No one could believe their eyes! It was a tie!

CHAPTER TEN

"I can't believe it!" Sharpay stared at the vote-tally board in shock. Then she whirled around to stare at Nathan. "This is all *your* fault!" she hissed. "If you hadn't voted for Troy—"

"Exactly," Principal Matsui interrupted. "Students, this is an excellent demonstration of why *every vote counts*. And I'm proud of all of you for coming out today and making your voices heard."

"Oh, who cares about voices being heard?"

Sharpay said impatiently. "No one *won*!"

Ryan waved his hand in the air. "We demand a recount!" he yelled. "Maybe that computer system messed up! Maybe a circuit board overheated or something!"

One of the computer techs who had created the board shot Ryan a dirty look. "The computer," he said icily, "does not mess up."

Troy turned to the principal. "Mr. Matsui, what does the tie mean in terms of the renovations?"

"Yeah," Chad said. "How will the school board decide who to give the money to?"

Principal Matsui furrowed his brow. "That's a good point. Actually, I don't think anyone made plans for this particular result."

"Let's have a runoff," Sharpay suggested, glaring at Troy. "I'm sure once East High students have a chance to think about their choices, they'll decide to vote for me."

"Bring it on," Troy said with confidence. "If some people switch their votes to you, I'm sure others will switch to my side."

"But then we'll just end up with another tie!" Taylor cried.

"And we won't get a better gym or a better auditorium," Ryan added.

Everyone stared at each other in frustration. Then Gabriella stepped forward and said, "Could I make a suggestion? I think there is a third option here. . . ."

"What are you talking about?" Sharpay said huffily. "Look at the ballot! There are only two things to vote for! One: auditorium! Two: gym!"

"Wait a minute," Principal Matsui said. "Let's hear what Gabriella has to say."

Everyone turned to stare at Gabriella. She felt her heart speed up, the way it always did when she was the center of attention. But she had an important point to make, so she took a deep breath and said, "Politics isn't supposed to be about winners and losers, or at least not all the time. It's supposed to be about compromise—figuring out the best way to help the most people, so that everyone gets a little bit of what they want."

What was Gabriella talking about? Sharpay shook her head in disbelief. She never settled for a little bit of anything she wanted. Sharpay wanted it all.

But Gabriella continued talking. "Sharpay wanted a concession stand for the auditorium. Troy wanted one for the gym. And Nathan—" She smiled at Nathan, and he almost dropped his armful of binders. "He was saying just the other day that it would be great to have a place to buy snacks in the afternoon, after the cafeteria closes."

"What exactly is your point?" Sharpay asked restlessly.

Gabriella ignored her rude tone and said calmly, "Why don't we use the money to build a concession stand that is halfway between the auditorium and the gym? That way, basketball fans *and* playgoers can get something to eat when they're at events, but all the other students will also benefit." She paused. Everyone was nodding slowly in agreement.

Everyone except Sharpay, of course. "But what about getting our dressing rooms painted?" she whined. "And our new lights?"

"And our new sound system," Eugene added wistfully.

"Who cares about your lights and paint?" Chad demanded. "What about fixing our floor?"

"And our banners," Zeke put in. "And the scoreboard."

"Wait a minute, guys," Troy said. "I think Gabriella's idea is great. And maybe we'd have enough money for each group to get one thing they wanted, in addition to the concession stand." He gave Principal Matsui an inquiring look. "Would that work, sir?"

The principal was beaming. "I'll have to crunch the numbers, but I think it's a real possibility!" he said. "Why don't we all meet in the library and see what we can figure out?" He turned to Gabriella. "Ms. Montez, I'd like to appoint you the mediator of the discussion. You've got just the kind of bipartisan approach that can really get things done!"

Gabriella was prepared to stay as long as possible to work out a deal. She was sure that Sharpay would argue against every suggestion and Chad would get angry, and that people's feelings would be hurt. But in the end, it was surprisingly easy to figure out a compromise that pleased everyone. After only an hour, she stood up with a piece of paper in her hand.

"Okay," she said. "I'm going to read what we've all agreed on. Ready?" She cleared her throat. "Instead of getting all-new lights, the Drama Club will get one new spotlight."

Sharpay gave a regal nod of agreement. "It *is* the most important light, after all!"

Gabriella continued. "Instead of an all-new sound system, they will get one new mixing board."

"Yeah!" Eugene gave two thumbs-up.

"And instead of having a decorator redo the dressing rooms, the basketball team will help the Drama Club repaint the rooms," Gabriella finished.

"Maybe we can even work off some detention while we're at it," Chad muttered to Troy.

Gabriella flipped to the next page of her notes. "The gym floor will be fixed, but the basketball team will have to give up the new scoreboard. And the members of the Drama Club will help make banners to hang in the gym and will work with the basketball team to paint the Wildcats' logo on the walls."

"Agreed," Troy said, grinning.

There was a pause. Everyone looked at everyone else.

"So, I'd like a show of hands," Gabriella said. "All in favor!"

Every hand went up.

"All opposed!"

No one raised their hands.

"Then we're done!" she said happily.

Everyone applauded.

"Now it's time to grab some pizza!" Chad exclaimed. "All this talk about politics has made me hungry!"

As the Wildcats picked up their backpacks and headed for the door, Troy saw that Sharpay and Ryan were hanging back.

"What are you guys waiting for?" he called out. "Come grab a slice with us!"

"Really?" Sharpay's voice was, for once, uncertain. "I mean, we did have a pretty hard-fought campaign—"

"And now we're working together," Gabriella said with a smile. "Come on. The sodas are on me!"

Something new is on the way!
Look for the next book in the Disney High
School Musical: Stories from East High series. . . .

RINGIN' IT IN

By N. B. Grace
Based on the Disney Channel Original Movie
"High School Musical," Written by Peter Barsocchini
Based on "High School Musical 2," Written by Peter Barsocchini
Based on Characters Created by Peter Barsocchini

Fresh snow blanketed the land around the Sky Mountain Ski Resort, the snowflakes sparkling in the sun. The sky was a bright, clear blue. The air was crisp and smelled like pine. It looked, Gabriella Montez thought, like a postcard—and the sight of the main lodge building brought back wonderful memories of her visit last year, when she had first met Troy Bolton.

As if Troy sensed what she was thinking, he came up behind her and said into her ear, "Want to sing some karaoke tonight?" When she turned to smile at him, he added teasingly, "Or would you rather hang out by the fire and read a book?"

"No way!" She laughed. "I'm not going to spend one minute of this vacation alone when I can hang out with my friends."

Gabriella looked past him to see other Wildcats chattering happily as they pulled their suitcases out of car trunks. What a difference a year makes, she thought. This time last year, I was sad because I was moving, all I cared about was studying, and I was sure I'd never make any friends as good as the ones I left behind. And now . . .

"Okay, guys, everybody count your bags and make sure you have everything!" Troy's dad, Coach Bolton, called out. "Then we'll check in and start having some fun!"

Everyone cheered. Troy's parents had come

up with the idea of organizing a group trip to the ski resort that the Boltons' had visited as a family for years. They had talked to other parents and before they knew it, the winter holiday break had suddenly become another fun Wildcat adventure. Mrs. Montez had been glad to sign up as a chaperone, along with Mr. and Mrs. Bolton. After a flurry of phone calls, Chad Danforth, Taylor McKessie, Zeke Baylor, Jason Cross, and Kelsi Nielsen got permission to come along.

"We won't get checked in for hours at this rate," Troy complained, nodding toward Sharpay and Ryan Evans, who were dragging luggage out of their limo. Sharpay had convinced her father that they had to drive in style. She had brought nine suitcases. They were all in the color she insisted on calling "Sharpay Pink" and were emblazoned with her initials. She was wearing a new pink ski vest, sweater, and pants. Her brother, Ryan, stood in the resort driveway. He caught Gabriella's eye and gave her a friendly wave.

"Ryan!" Sharpay snapped. "You're supposed to be in charge of our luggage!"

"I am!" he protested.

"Really? Because when we packed the car, I distinctly remember that I had nine pieces of luggage, yet I count only eight. . . ."

"Okay, wait." He dove inside, searched the backseat and emerged a few seconds later holding a small vanity case. "Here you go."

She nodded regally. "Very good. Now, let's check in and see what kind of upgrade we can get. I expect the Presidential Suite at the very *least*."

"I don't know about that, Sharpay," Chad said, as he grabbed his backpack from the backseat. "Isn't the Presidential Suite reserved for, you know, the president?"

Sharpay tossed her head. "Or someone *equally* as important," she said pointedly.

Hearing that, Taylor rolled her eyes and carried her suitcase over to where Gabriella and Troy were talking with Kelsi. "This was a great idea your parents had," Kelsi was telling Troy. "It'll be so much fun to ring in the new year in the mountains."

"Don't forget four days of hitting the slopes," Jason added.

"The snow looks great!" Zeke exclaimed. He had a snowboard tucked under one arm and an expression of eager anticipation on his face.

"I didn't know you cared about any powder that wasn't sugared," Chad joked. Zeke's love of baking had recently led him to an intense month of learning everything he could about making doughnuts.

"Hey, I like to get out of the kitchen once in a while," Zeke said. "In fact, I plan to pull off a 360 on this vacation!"

"And I'm going for a Backside 720!" Jason exclaimed. "I got close last winter. I'm sure I'll nail it this time. Come on, Chad! We can hit the slopes this afternoon if we get a move on."

"Oh, yeah, that would be great!" Chad said, a little too heartily. Then he glanced at the sky and added, "But I don't think we'll have time today. It'll be dark pretty soon, and the sky looks like it's clouding up. We may be in for a storm. . . ."

A young man standing nearby overheard their conversation. He had dark hair, bright blue eyes, and was wearing a Sky Mountain Ski Resort jacket. He strolled over to introduce himself. "Hi, guys," he said. "I'm Matt Hudson."

Before anyone could reply, Sharpay came running over. "Well, hi!" she cooed. "My name is Sharpay! It's great to meet you! Have you stayed here before?"

"Well, yeah." Matt grinned. "Actually, I work here. I'm a member of the ski-rescue team. Gotta pay my way through college somehow," he said.

"Really!" Sharpay exclaimed. "That sounds very heroic. And *so* dangerous."

"Do you have to rescue a lot of people?" Kelsi asked.

"It depends," Matt said. "Sometimes we'll see a lot of action, but other times it's pretty quiet. A big part of the job is letting people know how to stay safe and warning them about bad weather. That's why I wanted to talk to you guys. I know you just arrived, so you probably haven't heard about the storm we're tracking. It's supposed to come in tonight, so we're telling people not to go on the slopes until tomorrow."

"Oh, too bad," Chad said. "I was looking forward to trying out some new moves."

Gabriella shot him a curious glance. Chad didn't sound disappointed at all. In fact, he sounded relieved. Zeke and Jason looked a little crestfallen, but Troy shrugged. "Better safe than sorry. Anyway, there's tons of other stuff to do. Skating, video games, listening to music in the teen club—and, of course, there's always basketball!"

"A pumped-up, good-time dance party of a kid-friendly, Broadway style show"
Chris Jones, Chicago Tribune

Disney
HIGH SCHOOL MUSICAL
LIVE ON STAGE!

A NEW MUSICAL BASED ON THE
SMASH-HIT DISNEY CHANNEL ORIGINAL MOVIE

COMING TO A TOWN NEAR YOU IN 2008

BROMLEY • STOKE-ON-TRENT • NORWICH • EDINBURGH • YORK • WOLVERHAMPTON
WOKING • LEICESTER • SOUTHEND • NOTTINGHAM • BRADFORD • SOUTHAMPTON
HULL • BIRMINGHAM • MILTON KEYNES • WIMBLEDON • MANCHESTER
BRISTOL • NEWCASTLE • GLASGOW • LIVERPOOL • OXFORD
More dates to be announced

For dates and details visit www.HSMonstage.co.uk

GET YOUR VOTE ON!

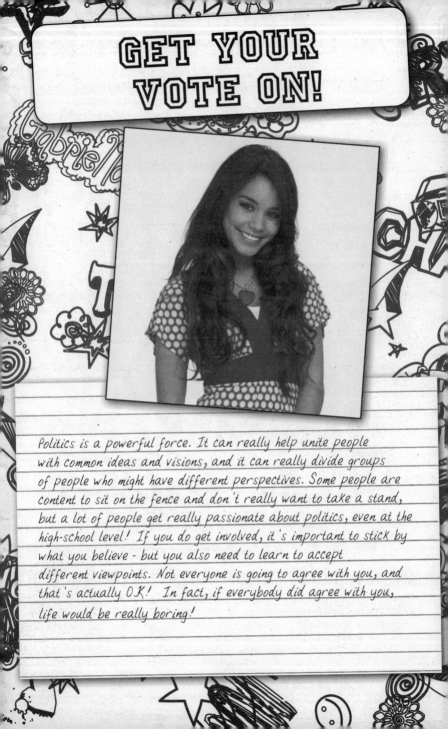

Politics is a powerful force. It can really help unite people with common ideas and visions, and it can really divide groups of people who might have different perspectives. Some people are content to sit on the fence and don't really want to take a stand, but a lot of people get really passionate about politics, even at the high-school level! If you do get involved, it's important to stick by what you believe - but you also need to learn to accept different viewpoints. Not everyone is going to agree with you, and that's actually O.K.! In fact, if everybody did agree with you, life would be really boring!

WHAT TEAM? WILDCATS!

For the Wildcats, nothing is more important than bringing the gym up to a standard that reflects East High's basketball success.

CHAD

The Wildcats are winners. We pride ourselves on working hard and keeping our heads in the game. But winners shouldn't have to play in a dumpy gym, but it's sad to say that that's what's happening right now. Don't get me wrong, I wouldn't want to play any place else — I'm a Wildcat for life! — I just wish our place looked as good as we do.

ZEKE

I DON'T LIKE TO COMPLAIN ABOUT STUFF, BUT THERE ARE 'DEAD SPOTS' ON THE FLOOR. QUITE A FEW OF THEM. WHEN THE BALL HITS ONE, IT JUST FALLS FLAT. AND THERE'S A PRETTY BIG DRAFT IN THE LOCKER ROOM. IT WOULDN'T BE A BIG DEAL, EXCEPT THAT WE PLAY A LOT OF GAMES IN THE WINTER, AND IT CAN GET REALLY CHILLY IN THERE!

TROY

There's a lot of history in our gym. My dad played in this gym. Somebody's granddad and great-granddad probably played here! It's an old, comfortable building, and no one wants to lose the history, but it's still time for a new court and bleachers, at the very least.

JASON

Troy's right. This place is super old. Sometimes, when I'm the last person heading to the locker room after practice, and it's totally empty and quiet, I swear I've seen a ghost on the other end of the floor, practicing free throws! We need a new gym and fast!

DRAMA CLUB SUPERSTARS

The Drama Club is led by Sharpay and Ryan, but the school productions are a major part of the school year for many of East High's students. Whether working backstage or in the spotlight, or just enjoying the show from the auditorium, this is the place that brings all the students together.

SHARPAY

Of course, the most important part of any auditorium is the star, like moi. The stage is important, too — that's where the actors practice their craft for all the world to see!" Our stage is a travesty. Boards squeak. There is tape leftover from productions that must have been a hundred years ago! The curtain has been known to get stuck. There is a tiny lip that I have tripped over more times than I like to count just as you exit stage left. The stage HAS to be redone!

RYAN

Sharpay is right, the stage could use some work. But the green room is in even worse shape. While the audience might never get to see it, this is where we all make costume changes and put on make-up, so it's pretty important, too. Some of the lights around the mirrors have never worked, it's either too hot or too cold, and don't even get me started on the condition of the actual costumes and props!

KELSI

A musical needs a lot of things to be successful, and one of them is definitely music. And for the music to be good, the musicians need good instruments, a good place to play and good acoustics. The acoustics in our auditorium aren't horrible, but they aren't really very good either. We have such talented performers that it doesn't matter too much, but it sure would be nice to get a new auditorium that helps the performances instead of muffling them!

GABRIELLA

I understand why Troy wants to see the gym renovated. It does need the work. But as everyone has pointed out, the auditorium needs just as much tender loving care, if not more. In a perfect world, the school board would approve the funds to fix both the gymnasium and the auditorium. Of course, in a perfect would neither one would need fixing! I hope Troy and his friends get the new gym they want, but I also can't help hoping that it isn't at the expense of the Drama Club.

ARE YOU A POLITICAL ANIMAL?

Some people just don't do politics, but everyone cares when it comes down to something that affects them directly. Find out who you compare to at East High by taking this test.

1. You read in the paper that your local community centre is going to be knocked down, do you...

A. FIND SOMEWHERE ELSE TO TAKE THE DANCE CLASS YOU ATTEND THERE EVERY WEEK

B. SEND AN EMAIL TO THE PAPER SAYING WHAT A SHAME YOU THINK IT IS THAT SUCH A POSITIVE CENTRE OF THE COMMUNITY IS TO BE DEMOLISHED

C. WRITE TO YOUR LOCAL GOVERNMENT TO COMPLAIN AND ASK TO HAVE THE DECISION REVERSED

D. GET ALL OF THE MEMBERS OF ALL OF THE CLUBS THAT TAKE PLACE IN THE CENTRE INVOLVED IN A MASSIVE PROTEST AND CALL THE PRESS ALONG IN THE HOPE OF GENERATING MASS MEDIA COVERAGE

2. A local, privately run 'no-kill' animal shelter is losing funding and about to close down. What do you do?

A. ADOPT AN ANIMAL. MAYBE TWO

B. RUN A BIG FUNDRAISER AT SCHOOL AND GENERATE AS MUCH MONEY AS POSSIBLE TO RESCUE THE SHELTER

C. DO RESEARCH TO SEE IF THERE WERE ANY GRANTS THAT THE SHELTER MIGHT BE ELIGIBLE FOR

D. GENERALLY I'M NOT A BIG FAN OF STRAYS. BUT IT WOULD BE A GOLDEN OPPORTUNITY TO CREATE A BUZZ ABOUT THE SHELTER BY INVITING EVERY NEWSPAPER AND MEDIA OUTLET IN TOWN TO A COMMUNITY MEETING ABOUT THE FATE OF THE SHELTER

3. The best way to change people's minds about something is:

A. TALK TO THEM DIRECTLY AND HONESTLY AND MAYBE EVEN BLUNTLY TO GET THE POINT ACROSS

B. HAVE AN HONEST DIALOGUE AND TRY TO FIND A HAPPY MIDDLE GROUND

C. IT'S HARD. BUT I DO MY BEST TO EXPLAIN MY POINT OF VIEW AND TO UNDERSTAND THE OTHER PERSON'S. TOO.

D. CONVINCE THEM THAT THEY ARE BEHAVING IN A STUPID FASHION: IF THAT FAILS. PUBLIC HUMILIATION ALWAYS WORKS

4. Your school is looking for someone to act as a student representative in governor meetings to help with decisions on funding allocation. Would you...

A. WRITE UP A LIST OF DISCUSSION POINTS FOR THE LUCKY STUDENT WHO IS CHOSEN FOR THE ROLE

B. VOLUNTEER IF THERE IS NOT ANYONE ELSE WHO WANTS THE POSITION. AN OPEN FORUM LIKE THIS IS A GOOD THING FOR STUDENTS. AND IT WOULD BE A SHAME IF NOONE WAS WILLING TO GIVE UP THEIR TIME TO MAKE IT HAPPEN

C. SUPPORT THE IDEA. BUT GLADLY LET SOMEONE ELSE TAKE A LEAD IN THE POSITION OF STUDENT REPRESENTATIVE

D. LAUNCH A CAMPAIGN TO GET YOURSELF SELECTED. IT'S ABOUT TIME SOMEONE LIKE YOU TALKED SOME SENSE INTO THE PEOPLE WHO RUN THE SCHOOL!

ANSWERS

If you answered mostly As, you're most like Taylor. You are a no-nonsense, pragmatic person who looks for solutions and believes in acting as independently as possible.

If you answered mostly Bs, you're most like Gabriella. You have a big heart and feel passionately about several issues and you are willing to do what you can to help.

If you answered mostly Cs, you're most like Kelsi. You pick and choose your battles carefully and generally like to do you part behind the scenes if you do get involved.

If you answered mostly Ds, you're most like Sharpay. When you get involved, you get involved, and you do everything you can to make your cause as big a spectacle as possible.

There's always room for improvement, especially at school, but sometimes we just get so used to things being the way they are that we don't think to suggest any alternative. Think about your school and what you would really like to change about it. Look at these other ideas from the students at East High, and then write a list of your top ten ideas for improving your school.

MARTHA COX

It would be nice if the science equipment got updated. I mean, my number one answer would be: build a dance studio with sprung floors, mirrors and music systems, but I just don't see that happening. So, science it is. The chemistry labs are older than Einstein, and with an awesome, powerful new telescope we could really get a chance to check out the stars

ZEKE

Obviously I'm with the rest of the guys: we need a new gym, pronto. But after that, a new lunchroom would be really nice. It's just high school lunch, so maybe it will never be gourmet, but I've been back there and it's not pretty! I think it should be illegal to use pots and pans that saw action in World War I! A new kitchen and new cooking equipment would really inspire the cooks — and they might even need someone like me to help them prepare some awesome desserts!

JASON

Whenever there's an away game, the Wildcats have to bus it to the other school and I have to say it - the buses stink. Literally! I'm sure they've been cleaned a hundred thousand times over the years, but they still kind of smell (probably from transporting sweaty athletes all over the place). So maybe East High doesn't need a new fleet of buses or anything that drastic, but it could sure use a few new ones. I mean, I've seen graffiti on the backs of some seats that might be Roman!

MS DARBUS

I realize that this was supposed to be a forum solely for students, but I would not be doing my duty as an influential faculty member if I did not weigh in briefly. Sharpay and Ryan have done a noble job campaigning on behalf of the Drama Club, and it seems clear that this cause is paramount to the needs of the school. What could be more important than introducing the young minds of our students to the theatre?

IMPROVE YOUR COMMUNITY

So, you've improved your school, now what? Well, you don't have to stop there. Here are a few suggestions East High students have for helping out in their community. See if any of these apply to your community and try to think of some more that you might be able to do yourself.

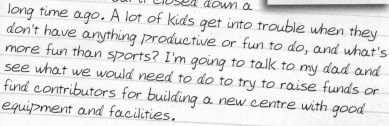

There used to be a recreation centre in town but it closed down a long time ago. A lot of kids get into trouble when they don't have anything productive or fun to do, and what's more fun than sports? I'm going to talk to my dad and see what we would need to do to try to raise funds or find contributors for building a new centre with good equipment and facilities.

There is a nice park in town, but it is always full of litter. I'm going to volunteer to help clean it once a week and see if any of my friends want to come along. What better place to start a grass-roots campaign than at a park!

I love animals, but I'm so busy with the Drama Club and just trying to keep my grades up, I know I don't really have enough time to get my own dog or cat. But that doesn't mean I can't volunteer to help out at the local animal shelter. They really need people to help walk dogs, and it would only be a couple of hours a week.

SETTLING POLITICAL DIFFERENCES

Some people say you should never talk to friends about politics, because it only causes arguments, but it's also a great discussion point which can help build and strengthen friendships. Either way, it's wise to tread carefully.

Sometimes you just need to accept that it's better to drop a discussion than continue, because you'll only end up feeling like you're banging your head against the wall. Here are a few red flags to watch out for that signal it's probably time to walk away:

1. You begin raising your voice and you just don't care. This usually means a cool discussion is quickly becoming a heated argument, and even if you are captain of the debate club, most heated arguments just end badly for all parties.

2. You and the other person might not be shouting yet, but you're both rudely interrupting each other every five seconds. So maybe it isn't heated, but you're not really having a productive discussion anymore. Either re-establish a ground rule that neither of you will interrupt again (not likely!) or agree to table the discussion until later.

. There is no heat, and there is no interrupting, but you notice that the other person has a very blank, zombified look on their face. Odds are, they aren't planning a witty rebuttal – they've just mentally checked out of the discussion. That doesn't mean you win. In fact, it might even mean that you were rude or failing to listen to the other person's points and they no longer see the use in debating. Either way, it's probably time for you both to walk, because you're just listening to yourself talk, and you already agree with you!

Sometimes you just need to agree to disagree, especially if friendships are involved. Just because you don't share the same opinions about things doesn't mean you're suddenly not as close or aren't good friends. But no matter what, don't let arguments get in the way of friendship. Here are a few tips about settling a disagreement when it just isn't possible to meet in a middle ground.

. You and your friend have both argued your cases, made all your points and you still find that you are worlds apart. There's a whole spectrum of thoughts on any political issue (and pretty much any other issue too!) and if you and your friend are on polar opposites, chances are no amount of arguing is going to persuade either of you to think differently. Time to agree to disagree.

2. Sometimes you have an argument with someone and you get the feeling that they really do realize that they might have been wrong about something, but they're just stubbornly digging in their heels to avoid admitting it. You might be tempted to say, "Oh, come on! You know I'm right!", but one of two things will probably happen: 1) You were wrong about them realizing they were wrong, and they just get more angry; 2) You were right about them realizing they were wrong, but they still get angry because you claimed they were being stubborn. Either way you'll never know and you should have just agreed to disagree and walked away when you had the chance!

3. You and your friend are heading towards a shouting match or fistfight. Definitely time to agree to disagree and head to opposite corners to cool off! There are probably a hundred reasons you and your friends are close – don't let one or two disagreements get in the way of all the good stuff!

Most people like to avoid confrontations (well, not everybody, obviously - some people don't seem happy unless they are causing a confrontation!). But that doesn't mean a disagreement has to be ugly or negative. In fact, you can learn a lot about each other by talking through something with an open mind and really trying to understand where the other person is coming from. You shouldn't abandon an idea or position if it is really important to you, but try to be flexible enough to really listen to an opposing position too. You might discover that there is more to an issue than you first thought!